EASY TO FALL

W. WINTERS

From *USA Today* best-selling author Willow Winters comes the epic conclusion to the heart-wrenching, romantic suspense series, Hard to Love.

With her I was always on the highest high. That's why it was so easy to fall.

I never stood a chance without her. The two of us were made for one another. It's as simple as that. The world could try to rip us apart, but it would fail.

Until this.

She told me once that love isn't enough. I never would have believed it…

I won't stop fighting. Not until the very end.

EASY TO FALL

Two words will help you cope when you run low on hope:
accept and trust.

—Charles R. Swindoll

PROLOGUE

Laura

They say death feels like falling. You plummet down to the center of a large black hole, blind with nothing to touch. Only a sinking feeling in the pit of your stomach and the rush of air around you makes you aware that the descent is happening. At first there's a dip in your tummy. The same kind of dip that happens on the road when you drive as quickly as you can down a hill. Like you're on a roller coaster. That same concoction of adrenaline and dread that forces you to either scream or smile in the face of what's instinctively fearful. And then it's gone and you're simply falling. That's what death feels like.

It's funny how similar that description is to falling in love, isn't it? There's no controlling it. You can keep your eyes open or you can close them. You can scream on your way down, or you can lift your chin and wait silently for what's about to greet you on the other side. Your death or a kiss.

Sometimes, it's both.

One or the other just takes a bit longer to happen, but you were falling all the while.

I didn't realize I was falling at the time, but now as I lay here, waiting for the end, I can pinpoint the exact moment when it happened years ago. I know the very moment I slipped and tumbled down.

Hindsight is twenty-twenty and all that.

I didn't even get a kiss when I started falling. One look at Seth King and I was done for. I've fallen many times since then, all those little dips that made me both smile and scream. Always for Seth. I guess you could say I died for him many times. But this time… this time will be my last. I know it will.

The difference between the two, love and death, is that you can come back from love. Death isn't as forgiving.

CHAPTER 1

Laura
Ten years earlier

"**Y**OU KNOW YOU CAN SIT WITH THEM IF YOU want," Cami tells me in between bites of her apple. It's just us on this side of the cafeteria table although at the other end on the opposite side, two freshmen girls are currently having a heated but hushed conversation. I guess they wanted privacy for their gossip and they've planted themselves on the very end of our table to get it. "You don't have to sit with me when you're dating Seth."

I shake my head in disagreement, my gaze moving from the brunette ponytail swishing behind one of the intruders at our table to Seth's table. Of course it's his. He owns it.

He smiles when he sees me. It's slow and charming, genuine too. The kind of smile where wrinkles form around his eyes when he does it. He's so damn handsome, it's not fair. How could I ever not want him? There's simply no denying it. My whole heart wants to beat with his.

That doesn't mean we have to put a label on it. I know damn well that it will be the kiss of death if we do.

And it sure as hell doesn't mean I can't sit with Cami anymore.

"We aren't dating," I say, denying what Cami suggests, even as my heart goes pitter-patter in protest. It's too warm in my chest, with too much commotion going on in there at the mere sight of Seth's smile. My eyes are caught by his steely gaze. There's a sense of tension and electricity between us. There's no use fighting it anymore.

"You're one of them now," she whispers, leaning closer to me for comedic effect with no trace of malice, only humor. And it works. I laugh, this ridiculously high-pitched laugh as my cheeks burn and I turn to her.

My lips part to object as I reach forward and unscrew the cap on my iced tea, but Cami doesn't give me a moment to form a rebuttal. "You hang out at the bar. You play pool with them. They walk with you on your way home."

"Not the whole way and not always," I protest.

She tilts her head and makes an expression like I'm being unreasonable denying it and maybe I am. In the last two months, I've spent every waking moment with Seth and his crew. And it feels like I belong there, like I was always supposed to be on that side of the room. It's like they're my new family. Not by blood but by choice. Cami is my family too, though. Nothing will change that. Ever. We will always be inseparable.

"Semantics," Cami argues and takes another bite of her apple. She doesn't bother swallowing before telling me with a nudge of her shoulder, "You should sit with your boy toy."

"Boy toy freaked me out a little yesterday," I say. I'm going off script, changing the subject and hiding behind huge news. I'm not sitting with Seth whether Cami's here or not. It would make what we have more real. And if it's real, it can be taken away from me. So my ass is staying put.

"What?" Cami's happy-go-lucky façade vanishes and she quickly glances behind me. "What happened?" she asks lowly, barely moving her lips as she keeps her eyes pinned to mine. I have to laugh, my shoulders shaking gently.

"Nothing bad," I start to tell her and my stomach does this weird flip that coincides with my heartbeat as I remember last night.

"So I was doing our biology homework last night, you know how there's that genetics question about kids? Like about what color eyes they'd have if both parents had blue eyes?"

Cami's in the middle of nodding and taking a sip of water when her eyes go wide, and she whips them to me. "Kids?" she questions, getting right to the point.

Again, my stomach does something strange, almost like it's cringing. Which is exactly what I feel like doing too.

"He said we'd make cute babies," I say and blush.

"Oh. My. God. Seriously, go sit with him," she says, brushing me off jokingly and then laughs. It takes her a half minute to completely change her tone. "You are not allowed to get pregnant in high school," she reprimands me although there's nothing but humor there. She knows how driven I am. Still… the thought, even if it was a quick one, of having a baby with Seth feels like the world shifting under my feet.

"As if," I half-heartedly joke and remember the next bit of the conversation. How Seth laughed, but it was a sad laugh, and then he told me he'd make an awful father.

I bet whatever it is that makes him feel that way is because of his own father. I never knew the man, not really. I only knew of him. Instead of replying to Seth's offhand remark, I simply kissed him. He told me, "You're too good for me, you know that?" Which earned him a quiet laugh and another kiss from me.

He's wrong about that. He's wrong about a lot of things, but one thing he's right about is that we would make cute babies.

Flip, tumble, I willingly fall all the way down…

CHAPTER 2

Laura
Present day

There's this sick feeling I get in my gut sometimes. It happens when I know I've messed up or when I'm highly aware that someone's going to be mad at me. My grandma told me once it's something that *people-pleasers* get. It's like this churning that's too deep and low to be due to my stomach but still wants me to throw up. Ever since I got off the call with Doctor Tabor, I've had that nauseated feeling.

I still have to go in for the ultrasound for more precise specifics, but the hormone levels in my blood are conclusive proof that this baby is farther along than a few weeks. She's sure of it. Months. Months and months. Not weeks along like I originally thought.

Suddenly, I'm even colder than I was just a moment ago and the blanket isn't helping. I don't cry. I won't cry even if my breath skips and hitches.

That revolting feeling churns again and I have to close my eyes. I haven't cried yet but I want to. *This baby isn't Seth's.* Just the thought makes my throat constrict and bitter tears prick the back of my eyes. I'm physically not all right. Not in the least.

Instead of giving in to the harsh need to let it all out in useless tears, I lean forward, picking up my cup of hot tea and take a sip. It's caffeinated and part of me thinks I shouldn't drink it because it means I'll just be staying up that much later. The other part of me thinks I shouldn't drink it because caffeine isn't good for the baby. But it's the only thing in this damn house that I can pretend will soothe me right now.

And that's all I'm doing. Pretending. Because nothing is all right. Not a damn thing. Rocking back and forth, my mind races and I try to work it all out in my head, but I can't.

I have an urgent need to get up and go to work. Not because I bury myself there when I want to run away... well, maybe partly that. But also because the answers I've been avoiding await me at work. I can reference the dates I went on by checking my old work schedules and I can make use of the equipment for pregnant patients.

I need to know exactly how far along I am. Hate and resentment burn inside of me, knowing I've been running all this while. I've known for weeks that I was pregnant.

Weeks! At the very least, I could have gone in at any point to make sure this baby was healthy. Instead, I was running from the truth and burying my head in the sand.

Seth's right, I do always run. I fucking hate myself right now.

My hand splays across my stomach as I stare out the window, watching a late-night thunderstorm crack open the sky with an occasional bolt of lightning. I pretend this doesn't hurt and that I'm not scared. And more than that, ashamed. Ashamed of being a horrible mother to this tiny life that hasn't even been born yet.

If it wasn't so cold, I'd slip outside onto the porch and listen to the sounds of the rain beating down on the roof. It's so soothing to hear. From in here, I can't hear the rain, and I can barely see it at all once the lightning ceases.

I haven't felt a single kick. I've barely gained any weight at all. In fact, my jawline is tighter than in recent months and my stomach only looks a little bloated. *If I'm really months along, I should be bigger.* Even as the thought hits me, I strike it down. Women carry differently. Every pregnancy shows differently. I need answers. I need to take care of myself and this baby.

Months. My chest pulses with pain as another burst of lightning rips the sky open. Thunder comes many seconds later. All the while my eyes are closed.

Months of drinking.

Months of stress at work and late nights.

Months of sex with various men. Only seven months ago I spent the night with one man and the very next night with another. Was I already pregnant then? *Impossible.* I can't be seven months along. No, no, I can't be that far along.

I need to know how far along I am and I need to know right now. Because the one thought that's been screaming in my head feels accurate. It feels right. *The baby isn't healthy.* No kicks, no weight gain. Maybe my heart is failing my child.

The tears prick again and this time one escapes and rolls down my cheek. I brush it away, pretending like it didn't happen and stare out of the window into the dark sky, speckled with blurs of the pouring rain.

I have work this week. Work will have answers. And I'll schedule every appointment my doctor wants first thing tomorrow. I just need to make it through tonight. *I'll be a good mom*, I silently promise my baby. I may fail everywhere else, but I promise I'll be a good mom.

More tears escape as I hold my stomach and I can no longer stop them.

I don't know how I'll make it that long. I can't take any more. From my heart, to Seth, to this pregnancy and jail. Jesus Christ! I can't take any more! My heart spasms in my chest and I grip at my shirt, stifling the useless sobs of self-pity. I've taken all my medication; I'm doing everything I can, but I can feel myself breaking.

So I do what I've done for years now. I pick up the phone and call Bethany.

It rings and rings. All the while I stare out of the window, watching the wind whip across the darkened tree line of pines. Something, anything, please take away this pain because my mind is going to the darkest of thoughts. How could it go to anything else? All my life has ever been is tragic.

"Hey, you okay?" Bethany answers, sounding slightly out of breath, which makes me lean forward, my comfortable blanket falling from my chest to puddle in my lap.

"Are *you* okay?" I stress, roughly wiping my face and getting a grip on my emotions.

"Yeah, just," she pauses and breathes out heavily before continuing, "yeah, I was just on the other side of the hall when my phone rang. I didn't put it on silent like an idiot."

"Oh," I say and settle back in the sofa, readjusting my blanket. "You have a minute?"

"It's bedtime over here, so I've got all the minutes in the world for you, love."

A smile lifts up my lips as I pick at lint on the blanket.

"I just… I have so much to tell you." A sadness washes over me at the realization that I haven't told her a damn thing. Secrets kill people. They bury themselves deep down where they hurt you but you can't feel it until the damage is already done. I should know.

My head falls back against the sofa as I stare aimlessly at the ceiling, feeling a hollowness of regret run through every inch of my insides. I'm always telling her to confide in me, yet I haven't let a soul in.

No one but Seth. And I can't tell him this.

"Yeah, I bet you do. You haven't told me anything," she answers and sounds of papers shuffling and slapping down on—probably the reception desk—come in through the background. It goes silent for a moment, then she sighs and says, "I feel like we've barely talked lately."

"I just…" I say and trail off, acutely aware I keep repeating this nonsense. *I just… I just…* I hate it.

"Where's Seth?" Bethany questions.

"He went out for a bit," I answer as if it's a normal night in the King household. Just like any other home. He went out for milk. He went out to pick up dinner. He went out to cache guns everywhere he could hide them and he might not come home. You know, *the usual.* The dread comes back and I squash it all the way down. There's too much else for me to worry about.

"Why does everything get worse and worse?" I ask her the rhetorical question, knowing I'm simply procrastinating and being a downer all the while. A thread comes loose on my chenille throw from my picking and I scrunch up my nose then put my hands under the blanket, resting them in my lap instead. Dammit. I love this blanket.

"What's going on? You're scaring me," Bethany replies in a single exhale.

My right hand travels to my stomach as another bolt of lightning illuminates the night.

With my lips parted and my eyes closed, I think of how I should tell her. It's so much to reveal. My heart. The pregnancy. How far along the pregnancy is.

An inhale, long and deep is what I give her, unable to tell her on the phone.

Why did I call, then? And when did I become such a chickenshit?

"Do you need me to come to you? I can call Cindy in." Her tone drops, becoming humorous as she adds, "I want to pay that bitch back anyway." A snicker leaves me.

"I... no. It's okay. I only needed to hear your voice. Guess I'm feeling a little bit lonely is all." *Chickenshit, chickenshit, chickenshit.* Although there is some truth to my statement. I feel very much alone right now.

"I can come right now, no questions asked." She would too. I know she would. It wouldn't be the first time one of us has dropped everything to help the other. Although in the past it's been because of her sister, or my unfortunate choice in men or alcohol, or both.

That's when the realization occurs. I have Bethany at the very least.

I always knew I could never really have Seth and if this is the last of it, of us, at least I have Bethany and so does this little one.

I should probably tell her about said little one before something bad happens.

"It can wait until tomorrow."

She heaves in a breath that sounds more like a sigh and says, "All right then. You should know I'm planning on passing the hell out when I leave here at five."

"Par for the course." I smile as I respond then take a sip of now lukewarm tea that doesn't do anything to soothe the ache in my soul.

"Love you," she tells me and I tell her I love her back.

I'll go to sleep and ignore these feelings. Tomorrow, when the sun is up and I'm able, I'll go to the doctor's and I'll take it from there. That's all I can do right now anyway.

Seth

My father always told me to trust my gut. He said there's something about humanity that tries to make us hide our baser instincts, but it's those instincts that keep us alive. Right now, I feel sick. I feel like something awful has happened. It's a hollowness in my chest. Not when I think about Marcus though, and not while Declan talks to me on the way to the corner store to meet with Walsh.

I may be headed to my death right now, but that doesn't affect me in the least.

It's when I look down at my phone and see Laura hasn't texted me back. That's when I feel like something's wrong. I don't know what it is, but I know something's wrong.

I try to convince myself that she's sleeping, but my gut tells me I'm a liar. There's something very wrong. The seatbelt across my chest feels tighter now and I can't get comfortable in this seat. She was fine when I left. I know she was fine, better than fine, even. Maybe worried but she always worries and this is the end to that.

The bright light from my phone pierces the darkness in the cab of Declan's car, getting his attention.

Love you, Babygirl. That was sent two hours ago.

"You all right?" Declan questions, turning down the radio station that was already barely on to begin with.

"Fine, just give me a minute." *Thump, thump,* something's wrong. I can feel it.

A quick call to the security team confirms she's inside the house, safe and sound.

"You sure?" I question Dominic and his confident voice reassures me she's inside, with no signs of distress. "Do you want me to go inside and check?" he asks and I tell him no. "Thank you," I say then hang up the phone. She was awake when I sent the text. They confirmed it.

The concerned exhale that leaves me gets an unsure look from Declan. With a fresh shave and a now empty orange energy drink that I can smell from here even though it's sitting in the console, he's wide awake and alert. "What's going on?"

I don't have an answer to his question.

Maybe it's just that I'm not ready to be a father. Maybe that's why I get this feeling every time I've thought about her tonight. Maybe I'm not used to telling her I love her and not hearing it back. There's some fucking karma for me.

"She's okay, right?" he questions as he readjusts his grip on the wheel. The motion is what I focus on as I shove the unwanted feelings aside.

"Yeah, Dominic said she's inside still and from what they can tell she's sleeping." *She probably didn't see it,* I lie to myself. She always checks her phone and plugs it in right before bed. Always. Laura is a creature of habit.

"Are you having second thoughts about this meet with Marcus?" he asks me as we roll by the Rockford Center, the large building and parking lot lit up while everything else has closed down this late at night.

The black leather under my ass groans as I readjust in my seat, staring out the window and listening to the rain beating against the car. The windshield wipers slide back and forth, clearing the way for more battering.

"No, no second thoughts. We need to end this and see what the hell he wants."

"It pisses me off. For months we've been trying to get in touch with him and no response. Then this?" It's quiet in the car as I stare at him, his anger attempting to disguise his concern. "If we had more time, we could go through the transcripts of their letters and have the upper hand."

The feeling vanishes at the mention of the letters. And just like that, my phone vibrates in my hand. *I love you too. Come home as soon as you can.*

She adds a moment later: *And in one piece.*

I may make her heart skip, but she does something to mine too. There's a sense of warmth and calm that hits me every time she says she loves me. I think it's because my heart knows she's telling the truth. She really does love me.

It's a fucking miracle that she does. An unjust one at that, but I'll greedily take it.

That stir of anxiousness leaves me instantly. She's all right. We're all right. *Damn, when did I become so insecure and self-conscious?* Oh yeah, the second she told me I'm going to be a father.

"Guessing your fight is over?" Declan asks, the cocky smirk on his face revealed easily via the light of my phone in the dark night.

"We weren't fighting."

"Whatever you say, King." Declan uses my last name when he replies, which is something he doesn't usually do. I notice it, but I don't know what to make of it.

He hasn't called me King in years.

I note how easy it is to shift my focus back to the point of this drive and tonight. Knowing Laura's all right, I can put everything into this meet with Marcus.

Declan's at ease, well as much as he can be. Letting the anger dissipate, he drives with one hand now as we pass the police station. Like the Rockford Center, it's brightly lit, a beacon in the barren streets.

Declan gives me yet another reason we should push off the meet. "We still haven't decoded all the letters."

"I bet that's why he wants to meet tonight, so we don't have time to figure out what they've been talking about," I comment, bringing the conversation back to Marcus, to the point of tonight's venture. It's far too calm now as we drive straight into the eye of the storm that is Marcus.

"That would make sense, which means technically, we do have the upper hand."

"Possibly," I say, correcting him. Absently, I tap my knuckles against the window, thinking back to every piece of information I was able to gather in the letters Walsh and Marcus wrote to each other.

"I wish they hadn't written the notes in fucking code,"

I mutter, pissed that it couldn't be as easy as simply reading them. Although there are literally hundreds of them, dating back for over a decade.

Declan's huff of a laugh lacks all sense of humor. "Tell me about it," he comments offhandedly, lowering his head slightly as he makes a left at the light.

"We know Marcus taunted Walsh at first but then they shared an interest in something."

"In what?" I question, wanting every piece of information. Declan had more time than I did to scour the letters. I only got a briefing and not a damn bit of it makes me feel prepared for what's to come.

"Killing a man who deserved it."

I swallow thickly, nodding. Marcus has always played a part in who lives and who dies in this town. Even Carter acknowledges that. The Cross brothers were never on Marcus's radar; the two men never had a problem that stirred between them.

That changed when Carter took Aria. That much is clear in the letters as well.

"Walsh said Marcus could have him." Declan's comment brings my attention back to him rather than what Marcus wrote about Carter.

"Who?"

"The man they agreed needed to die. It was a case, Walsh's case and he gave Marcus the green light to murder. That's when their friendship began and the letters came in more frequently."

"Right." I wonder if that's why Marcus wants Walsh there. "Maybe they're closer than we previously thought."

"Walsh said Marcus was an angel of death, a serial killer deciding who would live and die based on what they deserved."

"Do we trust what Walsh says?" I question Declan, who pauses. The windshield wipers are the only sound I can hear as we wait at the last red light.

"He's not wrong. He hasn't lied to us yet either."

"That we know of. But he's sure as shit held back."

"All I know is if Marcus is our moral compass, we're fucked," Declan comments.

"We take the train to the warehouse together. We take two trains back separately when we leave."

"At least your train is first," Declan says.

Nervousness pricks along my skin as I tap my thumb on my knee. This is it. An end to all this bullshit between Marcus and us. It fucking better be.

I have a child coming. A life I want to live. All this bullshit has to stop or else I know it will end the same as last time. I can already picture her leaving me. I will chase her to the ends of this world, but I won't let the danger accompany me. I won't let her be involved.

Marcus was wrong about Carter. He was wrong and he knows he was… it's in the letters. So he can go back to playing God and leaving us to our own devices. Or else… as Carter said last night, there will be a war.

That can't happen. Not again. I can't let that happen again. If it does, I will lose her forever.

"You all good?" Declan asks me and it's then that I realize we're here at the train station. "Ready?"

He parks the car on the left side, the tracks in front of us and empty spaces all around us. The night train leaves in half an hour.

A half hour, a twenty-minute ride, and then… it's the end of all this.

"Yeah," I answer him, "I'm ready."

CHAPTER 3

Laura

I T'S COLD. I CAN'T GET OVER HOW COLD IT IS. IT'S ALL-consuming, the freezing chill. My thoughts stay focused on it even as my surroundings come back to me. The stark white brick walls. The paint is so thick, like it's been coated a hundred times. The light is dim, because it's "lights out." That's right, I can't sleep. Not with Jean in here with me.

Shivers run down my spine. It's odd how I can't even focus on her lying across from me in her orange uniform. The one that matches mine.

All I can think about is how cold it is; the thin blanket in the jail cell simply isn't enough. Anxiety threads itself slowly through the thin fabric, followed by fear. So much fear. I can't sleep because if I do... she'll kill me. She's going to kill me. I know she is but still, my eyes close. I can't sleep, but terror *grips me. Exhaustion keeps me still, fighting against the need to sit up so she knows I'm awake. So she won't kill me. I can't die. I want to live.*

My eyes fly open, my heart galloping away at the sight of her. Taller, stronger, and more experienced in killing. Who was I to ever think I'd be a match? The terror is so encompassing that when she stands up, the blood dried around her neck and hands, I can't move.

Run! *I can't. I can't move.*

All I can feel is the pounding in my chest and the frigid cold along my skin.

Scream! Fight! Do something! *I can't do anything, though. I could never outrun this. I was supposed to die a long time ago. I'm living on borrowed time.*

My body's practically paralyzed, everything is so still and I'm about to be a victim as she makes her way to me.

Even when she pulls out her pocketknife, smiling at me, I'm trapped in a body that refuses to move. Her little nickname for me nearly forces me to close my eyes. Sickness coils in my stomach. I hate her and everything she stands for.

I stay still, as still as can be. All the while she waves the knife at me, giddy and proud. I can't move. I can't scream. I'm only watching.

Seth. Seth, help me. *I cry for him, even when I know he can't hear me. He can't save me here. Could he ever really save me? Wasn't I supposed to be the one to save him… and I didn't. I failed and now I'm going to die.*

I'm alone. So alone. All I'll ever be is alone.

Miraculously, my hand moves to my lower stomach.

Baby.

The soothing thought is only a word. I won't be alone. Tears fall down my face and that's when Jean smiles at me. You can't keep him, *she tells me, taunting me.* You don't deserve him.

Thump, thump. No! *Adrenaline scorches my blood as it races through me, challenging the pounding of my heart.*

Screaming. There's so much screaming.

It's all I can hear. My own voice screaming "no" as she closes the distance. But I still can't move.

And then both of us scream as she plunges the knife into my belly with one swift motion.

I jolt awake from the horrible nightmare and nearly vomit instantly. Somehow, I manage to keep it down, although my body shudders. A cold sweat bathes every inch of my skin as I sit straight up, my gaze darting around the empty room. My trembling hand covers my mouth and goosebumps line my skin.

Breathe.

I do just that.

Lift your shirt. See? It's okay. I go through the motions to prove it's a nightmare. Even with the fear lingering in my every thought.

It's only a nightmare.

It takes a long while for my heart to knock it off, and the fear to subside. Even longer to breathe normally.

Jean is dead. She's long gone. She will never hurt me or my child. Never.

One hand is still clutching the sheet with a white-knuckled grip and the other is protectively laid over my stomach. The light that filters in beneath the door from the hallway is the only light I've got besides the clock on Seth's nightstand. The digital numbers read 3:15.

One breath in and then another. It takes a moment to steady myself, but I do.

Blinking away the little bit of sleep I got, I finally notice that Seth isn't home. He's been gone too long. My first instinct is to check my phone and I'm glad I do. He texted me an hour ago saying that there was a delay. A few minutes later, he messaged that he hoped I was sleeping.

"I wish I were sleeping too," I mumble, rubbing my tired eyes. My shoulders shake with a shiver that won't quit. Sighing out the frustration, I rip off the covers and go to the bathroom to take my pills. Four of them, every morning, for my heart. And then a prenatal vitamin.

I've never taken so many pills in my life. It's a bit early to take them, but there's no way I'm going back to sleep. Not after… that.

I wash my face and when I do, the vision of Jean comes back, only this time I'm saddened by it. By the memory of what happened and what I did. I suppose I'm not over the fact that I killed her. With the water still running, I lean my weight forward and rock slightly, gripping the porcelain sides of the sink.

I did what I had to do. And I can live with the nightmares if they're my consequence. I accept it.

It isn't the worst nightmare I've ever had. It isn't even

the worst thing that's happened to me, murdering someone in cold blood—it's not even the most frightening thing. If I just ignore it, the nightmares will go away. I nod at that conclusion. It's true. I've been here before with worse terrors. This isn't the most horrific thing that's happened to me and it won't be the last event of my life that gives me night terrors. Well… so long as I live long enough. A sarcastic chuckle comes paired with an eye roll.

I'm not giving up on my heart just yet.

I'm just not myself. Right now, I am not myself at all. But I'm okay. The baby's okay.

My thoughts eventually give way to a whispered mantra. "The baby's okay. The baby's okay." It's the only thing I can repeat that calms me down. The adrenaline, the chills, the fear—it all means nothing because my baby is okay.

My gaze rises to the mirror, where dark circles under my eyes greet me.

I can't stand to look at them or the redness gathering in the whites of my eyes. I can't get back into bed either. Not with the nightmare still fresh over the sheets.

One look at the rumpled covers and I have to turn away before her voice hisses in my ear again.

I tell myself I'm just getting tea and then I'll climb back in bed, but that doesn't explain why I grab a thick sweatshirt and throw it on over my pajamas. I know my boots are at the door.

I was always a bad liar, even to myself.

I told Seth I'd be here when he got back, but I can't stay. I need to get out of here. I still have time to catch Bethany before she leaves at five, the start of the morning shift. Work will be slow and I have to tell her.

I'll bring her a cup of coffee so she can power through this next hour—that last hour is a bitch, after all. It's always the most boring, just doing rounds on patients as they sleep.

The rain from earlier has stopped, but I still manage to walk right into a deep puddle the second I make it down the porch steps.

"Fuck," I mutter as the freezing cold water splashes up the right leg of my pants and I curse my way to my car in the cold night. My breath fogs in front of my face and all the while my keys jingle happily beside me.

The radio's on when I get in my car and I'm quick to turn it down. The car starts with a rumble and I sit back in my seat, digging my phone out from my purse.

I'm smart enough to at least let Seth know where I'm going. He doesn't get a say in whether or not I go though, given his ass isn't even here.

I whisper the text as I write it out in my phone, "Getting Cami coffee and going to the center. I'll be back before six to go back to sleep." I nearly send him the message when I realize my mistake.

Cami.

I wrote Cami.

Fuck, that pain is sudden and fresh. It's a familiar pain of loss I haven't felt in a long time. *Fuck.* My head slams back against the headrest.

I could tell myself I'm just tired, but that's not all this

is. I miss her. I miss her so damn much with everything happening. Cami would know what to do and how to tell Seth the truth. Damn it hurts and forces more tears to well up in my eyes. I wish Cami were here. "No more fucking crying," I mutter to myself.

A sharp pain that feels like a knife twisting in my chest makes me struggle to take in a steady breath. My eyes close tight and my neck arches back so my face is toward the hood of the car. I cover my face with my left hand and drop my phone into my lap. "No more crying," I whisper into my clasped hands. "My baby is okay and I can't cry because it'll upset the baby," I say. Making the bold statement helps me. It truly calms me through and through.

With a shuddering breath, I admit I'm all sorts of fucked up this witching hour, but I change *Cami* to *Bethany* and hit send, gathering my composure and continuing with this plan I've barely put together in my head.

I pull out of the drive before Seth can text back and tell the men at the gate where I'm going.

There are two men on security duty in the brick shack at the end of the drive. At least that's what I call it; although I'm sure it's armored and reinforced to high heaven, I still call it the security shack in my head every time I look at it. With a single look at each other, they decide which one will follow me and tell me to wait until he's behind me.

Security detail is still a thing, I guess. This time it's a man named Garett with dirty blond hair that looks charming like it is even though it's all messed up. He also looks far too awake for 3:00 a.m., but I don't question it. I only nod and sit there in silence, waiting for him to get the car. I don't care if Seth wants them to follow me for the rest of my life, to be honest. They can follow me through the coffee shop drive-through that's open twenty-four hours all they want.

Which Garett does.

Follow me wherever. Just don't tell me where to go.

The entire ride is silent. My stomach bothers me and it grumbles. Right before the turn to the center, I swear I feel a bump or a kick, but I can't tell for sure. I hold my breath as I turn in and all the while that I'm idling, my keys still in the ignition, my car still running and the smell of a large mocha coffee and a large hot chocolate still permeating the small space, I wait for another kick.

But the kick, if it was that, doesn't happen again. I swear I felt it though. A little hope stirs in my chest.

I rack my brain trying to remember when kicks start as I put the car into park, absently noting that there are three other cars parked here. Two of them I recognize as Aiden's and Bethany's. Kicks start up earlier for some women, like within two months. Others around four or five months, I think. So that doesn't do me a damn bit of good.

I fight the urge to rub soothing circles on my tummy as I make my way into the Rockford Center. Mostly because each hand is grasping a foam cup of hot liquid.

Gesturing to the handsome babysitter, also known as my security detail, I motion that I'm going in as he parks his car and I hit the handicap door button on the exterior of the building for the front entrance to open for me.

My memory is shit this early in the morning but I still wish I'd paid more attention to the maternity chapters of all the textbooks I've had to read and all the classes I've had to take. One thing though that always stood out is that every woman is different, so therefore every pregnancy is different. Which doesn't offer me any comfort as I take the elevator up. Not a damn bit.

Nerves build in my belly as the elevator rises one floor at a time.

Ding.

The elevator arriving is the only noise on the entire floor. It can be unsettling this late at night, with the hallways empty and the lights on overnight mode, so they're off until motion is detected. It's creepy as fuck, to be honest.

Luckily, the main light is always on since someone is always here.

The view of Aiden leaning out from his office is a welcome sight, even if the look on his face isn't.

With his brow furrowed he asserts, "You aren't on the schedule for today." *Well, that's a nice hello.*

"I know," I answer him, shrugging off my coat at the reception desk and laying it on a cleared-off spot free of fall décor and paperwork. The cold still clings to me, so I pick the hot cup back up the second I can. "I just brought Bethany coffee."

"She should be done with her rounds in a few minutes." His answer is simple, welcoming even, but his face is still pinched with concern.

"Are you all right?" he finally questions and I give him

an honest answer, saying, "I couldn't sleep and something's been bugging me that I thought Bethany could help me with."

I half expect him to tell me that now is not the time, don't bring personal life into work, blah, blah, blah, but he only nods once and tells me, still leaning just outside his office door, "If you ever need anything, I'm here." It's sincere and his tired eyes reflect nothing but genuine warmth.

"Thanks." The word leaves me a little too quietly and I have to clear my throat before I can say it louder.

With a pat on his door, he vanishes back into his office, the door being left open just an inch. *Nosy fucker...* The snide thought does nothing but lessen the tension in my shoulders and put a smirk on my lips. I do like that nosy fucker, even if he's been weird lately. I've been weird too, after all.

The moment I pull up an extra chair beside the one behind the reception desk, Bethany's there.

"What the hell are you doing here?" It's nearly an accusation, probably the exact words Aiden wanted to say. With her wide eyes riddled with concern, she smiles back when I smile up at her, holding out the hot cup of coffee.

"Brought you coffee and a dilemma that won't let me sleep." Inwardly I grimace, remembering the real reason I woke up. I imagine Jean will haunt me for the rest of my life and I sure as hell will never breathe a word of what happened to anyone. *No Jean. No nightmare.* But this early morning, before the sun has a chance to slip out, I'm telling Bethany everything else.

All the tension leaves her squared shoulders and she eagerly accepts. The clipboard she held in her hand claps down on the desk as she sinks into the chair beside me and takes the coffee with a grateful simper.

With her pink scrubs bunched up her arms, she blows across the top of the coffee and takes a sip. With the steam pouring out of the small opening at the top, it must still be too hot because her sip is short and Bethany's a girl who gulps down a drink, rather than savoring it.

I fidget in my seat, twisting the chair back and forth and waiting for the right words to come, but they don't.

An easy hum of satisfaction from Bethany is followed by the easy demand as she says, "Spill it."

Thump. My heart slams in protest, but I ignore it. It wants to fight everything nowadays.

"I have a heart condition and it's worse than I ever could have imagined."

Bethany's demeanor changes in a blink. Setting her coffee on the desk, she leans forward, the blood draining from her face.

"Okay," she says, in the tone we use when talking to patients, although fear drowns the neutral word. She looks like she's about to break down and she expects me to tell her I'm going to die. Which… I would, if I were to be completely honest.

I pick at my nails, feeling this wave of heat roll up my body.

"I'm on the donor list for a transplant because surgery is too risky."

"Oh my God," Bethany blurts out and covers her face, her body crumpling in on itself but only for a moment. She's quick to correct her posture and reach out a hand to me, which I accept. Her hand holding mine, just a little human touch, is everything that I needed.

"I'm not concerned about that as much as something else."

"What the hell?" Her answer comes out in a single breath. "You need to be," she adds and she's harsh with her rebuttal, tears gathering in her eyes and falling just as quickly.

"What can I do?" I say and shake my head gently. "I have medicine, I take it. And now I wait. Why concern myself when there's something more important?"

Her bottom lip wobbles for a fraction of a second before she rakes her hand through her hair, pulling her hand from mine, and starts listing everything else I can do. "Diet, stress levels, there's so much you can do."

"Is there really though? I'm doing the best I can with it, but we both know sometimes it's not ..." I trail off and swallow thickly before continuing. "I promise you, I'm doing everything the doctor told me and praying for a donor match to become available so I can have the surgery." As Bethany nods in understanding, although I'm not sure she believes me, I watch her swallow and promise myself I won't tell her the doctor only gave me a year. I'll lie if she asks. She doesn't need to know that. I accept whatever comes to me on this front. I'll do everything I can, but I've prepared myself for death before and I can't run any longer.

"I'm also pregnant," I blurt out before the sadness overtakes this entire conversation.

"What?" she exclaims and I practically chuckle at the whiplash Bethany just went through.

Her eyes are wide and her expression simply shocked until I tell her what she needs to know.

"I'm pregnant and I'm so happy," I say although my voice cracks during the last part and I hate it. "Why do I keep crying?" There aren't tears yet but I swear if they come I'll be pissed.

"Because you're pregnant," Bethany answers as she gets off her chair to hug me. Her embrace is steadying, just like I knew it would be. A safe place full of shared happiness and love.

"All these tears," I say, wiping at my eyes to keep them from coming and then wiping my hand on my pajama pants. She takes that as her cue to sit back down, although she doesn't take her eyes off of my stomach.

"It's because you're pregnant," she says again, sniffling and plucking tissues out of the box on the reception desk. She hands one to me and keeps another for herself.

"Oh yeah? Then what's your excuse?" I jokingly push back.

"Because *you're* pregnant," she says comically, quietly laughing and I join in with her.

After the laughter dies down, the realization slowly hits her. "How is your heart going to hold up with…"

"The doctor wants to do a planned cesarean to avoid the stress of labor."

It's a sobering thought once again, but I keep a thin smile plastered where it is. I won't let this light be dimmed. My baby will be okay. My baby *is* okay. That's what matters right now.

"I …" I pause and take a deep breath, hating the next part. "I don't know how to tell Seth—"

"He'll be so happy," she says, cutting me off, so certain that I'll get to have that part of a happily ever after. She reaches for my hand and I pull away, shocking both her and myself.

"Sorry, it just hurts." I swallow thickly before continuing. "Because he *was* happy, when I told him." Confusion mars her tired eyes until I add, "But I just found out that this baby isn't his."

Bethany can't tear her eyes from mine, not even as she reaches for her coffee as if it will protect her from the uneasiness of this conversation. Tears cloud my vision and prevent me from clearly seeing the shock on her face.

"Do you know who?" she asks and I shake my head.

"I literally have no idea. I always used protection. I may have been a little … promiscuous… but I wasn't reckless." The defensiveness in my tone isn't needed. Bethany's never judged me. She never would.

"I know you did. I know."

"I have my schedule from the past few months in the office and I can look through it to see the dates." She nods along with my explanation.

"I want to tell him but I have to go to an appointment first to make sure everything is okay. To make sure the baby is healthy and find out exactly how far along I am."

"You haven't gone to a doctor?" Her question doesn't hide her shock and how ludicrous she must think this situation is. "You just went. I went with you! You were right there." I squirm in my seat. There's that shame again.

"I didn't realize I was pregnant. Definitely not this far along—"

"How far?"

"I don't know… That's partially why I'm here." I glance down the hall, past Aiden's office, where I know there's an ultrasound machine.

I don't even have to tell Bethany what I'm thinking before she grabs my hand, her ass already out of the seat as she says, "Let's go see your baby."

CHAPTER 4

Seth

"H E SET THE MEET, HE SHOULDN'T BE LATE," Walsh mutters without breaking his steady pace. He hasn't been still since we got on the train.

Nervousness keeps him pacing in slow but steady circles around a staircase in the center of the nearly empty warehouse. It's driving me fucking crazy. Maybe this is what Marcus wanted… for me to kill Walsh before he gets here.

Letting out a controlled exhale, I slip my hands in my pockets and glance past the iron rails of the staircase to the large, sleek silver doors of the elevator behind it.

"It's always a warehouse," I murmur so low, Walsh doesn't hear.

He stops in his tracks. "What?" The fact that we're both in suits doesn't mean shit right now. Exhaustion is evident on his face and I can feel it weighing down my own expression. I don't have to see myself in the reflection of the elevator doors to know I look like hell.

Pinching the bridge of my nose, I tell him, "Nothing."

"He's never made me wait before," Walsh tells me then takes a few steps, walking closer to the edge of the room where boxes are stacked. "He's always waiting. I bet he's here. Just waiting."

This place must still be in use, which makes me think there are cameras, although I haven't seen one yet.

I've gone over how to phrase everything we need to discuss so that if there are security cameras here, I won't be implicated if footage turns up later.

I don't trust Walsh. I don't trust Marcus.

At this point, an hour past the time agreed upon for the meet, I don't trust my gut either. It told me to come, and now it's screaming for me to leave.

"Seth King." A deep voice booms from somewhere to my right through the barren warehouse. The familiar chill that comes with it travels up the back of my neck.

Marcus.

Just his name irks me, so the sound of his voice feels like someone digging even deeper into a fresh wound. "Finally we meet," Marcus states, but the voice comes from the left this time. Nervousness travels down my spine, starting at the base of my neck.

"Is that what this is?" I question, keeping my voice even

and letting my gaze roam from the left side of the room to the right, slowly going over every shadow and stack of boxes. There are three levels, with the main floor open all the way up to the third floor with a railing along the hallways that line each floor. The building itself is at least thirty feet high. In this tin can of a warehouse, Marcus could be anywhere. "Usually when I meet someone, I see them," I add, raising my voice and feeling my spine straighten, my shoulders squaring.

The voice, in response, comes from behind me. "Did you really think I'd allow that?"

Walsh turns to face the sound, irritation clear on his expression, not the fear I imagine Marcus intended. I don't follow suit. My feet stay planted right where they are and I force myself to remain in control. Despite everything he's done, Marcus is only a man. "Yes." My voice is strong and every emotion except for irritation flees. "I did think you'd meet me face-to-face."

Everything Marcus does is deliberate, and I'm sure not showing his face is part of his plan, but also this theatricality with scattering his voice was done for a reason.

"I'm not entertained," I add.

"Then you're more foolish than I thought and perhaps I've made a mistake."

"Was it meant to frighten me, Marcus?" I question him, walking toward a pallet of stacked boxes in the corner. There are wooden toys inside of them. Little knick-knacks that toddlers would play with. Over here, the light is scarce, making it more difficult for him to see me... I presume. "Or did you want me to be aware that you don't trust me?" I ask a bit lower, not bothering to raise my voice this time.

As I open a lone box lying behind the stack, I peer at Walsh from my periphery. He stays where he is, leaning against the rail and waiting patiently. Both his hands grasp the rail behind him while he watches the elevator doors.

"Have you done this before?" I direct my question at Walsh, who stares down at me since I'm now crouched. "Come to meetings with Marcus that are more of a show than anything?"

"It's always a show." Walsh's response is easy, although his expression is anything but. I respect the man at least for that.

"I can see you're frustrated," Marcus answers, his voice coming from a level above and to my right. The light doesn't reach that corner. "I never had any intention of showing myself to either of you. You should know that. You are a smart man, Seth."

"What are your intentions?" I ask. Walsh's footsteps clack on the concrete floor as he walks closer to me, where he could get a view as well. There's nothing to be seen from the corner on the second floor, but the next time Marcus speaks, there is no sign of a speaker or any device. It's him.

His voice bellows down from the second floor as he says, "I have a proposition for each of you, and I'm scarce on time." He must signal someone, because a thick shadow shifts in the distance. It's the only sign of movement.

There he is. Still hidden, but there nonetheless.

"You know how to reach me," Walsh says carefully.

"Our form of communication has been compromised," Marcus admits from upstairs and Walsh's brow furrows.

"Isn't that right, Seth?" Marcus's voice is accusatory.

"We found your letters, if that's what you're referring to." Heat dances along the back of my neck and my palms itch as Walsh's gaze moves to my form. I don't take my eyes from Marcus though. Or rather, where I know Marcus is.

"Where at?" Walsh questions and I answer, still not averting my gaze although I can feel Walsh's piercing mine.

"The post office."

"You could have told me on the way over so I didn't feel like a dumb prick," he mutters beneath his breath for only me to hear. The anger is temporary.

"We have other ways," Walsh speaks to Marcus.

"I don't trust them any longer," comes the reply. Marcus's harsh and darkened voice seems... tired, resigned even as he talks to Walsh. He corrects it as he raises his voice to say, "I thought you'd like to hear this as well. It's quite interesting, if nothing else."

My pulse quickens as my palms sweat. Waiting for whatever it is to come, still, I can't hold back a line I've been rehearsing in my head the entire silent train ride here.

"You made a mistake targeting the Cross brothers. We know you know that. You admitted it in the letters."

Walsh peers at me, his head dropping and I note that

he stares at the floor as I speak. As if considering what I'm saying, debating whether it's true or false.

Marcus's silence urges to me to continue. "They don't need to be on your list. All we want is to go back to our former relationship."

"That's not going to happen," he says and Marcus's response only makes my hackles rise. Anger stirs in my blood.

"Then what is it you want?" I question, my voice coming from deep in my gut. "War?" I hate him in this moment. A bloody battle is the last thing I want.

His answer hits me hard in the chest, not just surprising me, but instilling a new fear. "To save Laura."

"Don't you fucking dare mention her name," I say and the sneer leaves me before I can think twice. Fists turn my knuckles white and I step closer to the edge, hating that he's not on this floor.

"You can't play God," Walsh bites out.

"I'm not," Marcus answers. "God has mercy."

"Don't you touch her," I say and I don't bother to hide the threat in my snarl.

"I don't plan on it. Let me explain."

"Explain," Walsh pipes up, reaching out for me. Not holding me back, but simply putting out his arm as if to stop me. There's nowhere for me to go, no way to get to him from here.

A new terror binds me in place at knowing she's anywhere near this man's radar.

It takes everything to be silent as my vision turns red.

"You had what I had. On the West Coast, you had control and power. The streets whispered your name like they do mine here. So naturally I had to keep an eye on you."

He pauses, although I don't know why or what he expects from me. All I keep thinking is that the moment he mentions her name again, I'll kill him. I will find a way to kill him.

"It became very clear that you followed her to the East Coast. Laura Roth. Love is so unpredictable. While everything else is… easily controlled."

"I'm warning you." My voice is barely contained. A deep-seated fear of losing her takes over. It claws at my stomach, tearing up everything inside of me. I don't let it show. Not an ounce of it. But I can't react either. I can't speak or else he'll hear it. He can't know.

"I want to save her." Marcus repeats what he said before and my head drops.

A sick, twisted smile lingers around the threat that leaves me, keeping the words steady as I say, "If you kill her…"

"I won't."

"Is she a target? Who's going after her?" My voice holds nothing but a menacing tone. All I need is a name.

"You should talk to her," he says and Marcus's easy response angers me even more. "Seth, she isn't well."

Questions race in my mind while emotions run through me. Is it a threat? Is that what this is? Does he know she's pregnant? Does he think there's something else going on with her? What the fuck does he mean by, "she isn't well?" My mind races and I can't stop it from going to the darkest of places.

As if reading my mind, he speaks, "It's more than her pregnancy. You'll see."

"You're lying." I hiss the response and oh so subtly, Walsh nods in agreement with me. His gaze is fixed on the spot where Marcus remains hidden.

"She'll tell you. I have faith that she will."

"Fuck you!" I can't control the chaotic response and Walsh grabbing my wrist is the only indication I have that I've stepped forward once again. "Stay away from Laura," I warn Marcus while shaking off Walsh's grasp.

"I have a way to save her." Marcus's voice is calm and at his admission, Walsh's expression turns quizzical. He stares into the darkness as I glance between the two of them. "And I promise you," he says, his voice becoming easy, like it was earlier with Walsh, "I have no intention of going anywhere near her or hurting her."

The pounding of the blood in my ears calms me. *Save her.* I would beg on my knees for him to save her if I truly thought he could. Or that he would. Or if she truly needed saving.

"I see you're skeptical," Marcus says, "but I've made the gathering of valuable information my life's work. I see everything, even things I don't care to see." He practically whispers the last line.

"What do you want from me?" I question him, my eyes narrowed.

I can practically hear the smile in his voice as he says, "I want you to owe me something."

"Tell me what you want," I say, pushing for him to get on with it.

"Walsh," Marcus says in a way that causes chills to roll down my arms, "this is where it gets interesting."

CHAPTER 5

Laura

"So… if the baby isn't Seth's?" The small room is far too sterile for this conversation. "How do you think he'll react?" she says and I take in a deep steadying breath.

Bethany gives me a moment to think up an answer, glancing between me and the tall machine in the room with the monitor that I can't take my eyes from.

The ultrasound gel is being warmed up, the machine is on and a textbook is open next to the keyboard on the desk for Bethany to reference.

I answer honestly, "I don't know." I genuinely have no idea how he'll react. But I know it'll crush the happiness he had. I'm all too aware of it.

Laying my head back on the small and thin disposable

pillow, I listen to the rustling of the paper under my ass. I opted to take off my pants and I still have my shirt on, just lifted. Aiden better not come in here or he'll get an eyeful, that's for sure.

"I'll have to go through the dating apps I had and the schedule I kept to even narrow down who the father is." My throat is tight at the confession and shame forces my eyes closed. "I should at least know that before I tell him, I think." I nod with my eyes closed, as if agreeing with myself. "I should know everything before I tell him."

Bethany doesn't agree with me and neither does the pang in my chest.

It's quiet for a long moment and in that time I envision the conversation. I can barely stand the imagined sight of his sadness and disappointment. He wanted this. He was elated when I told him. My throat gets tight and I have to open my eyes to stare at something else, anything else. I can't take this baby away from him. It's going to hurt him. No matter the details, I know it's going to destroy him… and us.

"Okay, hold on." The sound of Bethany flipping a page in the textbook makes me turn to her. "You know we could wait for Sheila to come in tomorrow?" she says, but she doesn't take her eyes from the book.

"I don't want anyone to know until I know."

Insecurity runs rampant on Bethany's expression. "It's been so long since I've done this and I don't want to fuck this up," she practically mumbles.

"Just do it. We have to hurry anyway before Aiden realizes I stole you away."

"Cindy can cover for me. She should be here any minute now." She stares at the textbook, reading something rather than looking at me and my pleading expression for her to hurry the hell up.

"Cindy can't cover her own ass." I keep my tone light and so does Bethany with her response: "You're not wrong."

My chuckle is silenced by the squeeze of a bottle and gel plopping onto my exposed stomach.

"I think there's a bump," she says and Bethany's voice holds a hint of awe as she stares down at my tummy, now covered in goo.

"You're going to regret that if all of this is a mistake and I'm not really pregnant."

Neither of us laugh because she puts the transducer right beneath my belly button. Neither of us do anything at all other than stare at the monitor as the black screen turns to white streaks that resemble the waves of an ocean as they crash on the shore. The wand moves to the right and still nothing. There's no little blip. No sign of life and fear cripples me.

There's no little sac, there's nothing.

Not until the wand is moved to the left and at what I see, my hand reflexively covers my mouth.

"There's the baby." Bethany's sweet voice is all singsong and happy and I can't say anything at all. I'm too choked up.

My eyes burn with happy tears at the sight on the screen. I can't think of a single time, in my entire life, that I've ever cried happy tears. Not until today.

There's a flicker on the screen. A little tiny one right where the heart would be and it's in tune with a steady rhythm that comes through the speakers.

"It sounds like a little train," I whisper, listening to the *chugga, chugga, chugga, chugga* that is so steady and perfect. So perfect. *Please don't have a heart like me, little one.*

With my bottom lip unsteady, I get hold of my bearings enough to ask Bethany, "Is that you moving the wand or the baby moving?"

"That's just me. It looks like the fetus is sleeping." Bethany's eyes are glossy, but she keeps it professional. Still she whispers, "You're having a baby."

It's okay that there's no movement yet. Everything's okay because of the *chugga chugga*. Even so, I want to see him or her move. Some other sign. I want all the signs, if I'm being honest. Every sign in the world that this baby is okay and I didn't unknowingly hurt him or her.

Just like that, the little baby moves. He—or she— moves. I see it!

"Maybe that was a kick?" Bethany questions, obviously as thrilled to see the leg jolt like that as I am.

"I can't feel it." I shake my head.

"It's different for every pregnancy and mother. There's nothing wrong with that," she says, ever reassuring.

"I know, I know." I can't look at her. I watch my baby all the while. I barely even register the word until she starts moving the wand again.

Mother. She referred to me as a mother.

A tingle spreads down my skin and I can't move my

eyes away. That's what I am, a mother. My head lays back, easier this time, waiting to see if the baby will kick again. I can see the legs, the arms, the big ole head and forehead. There's a little baby, a little life, inside of me.

Bethany never stops moving the wand and I wish she would hold still over his or her precious face. I want to see my baby. My first thought is that I want to see if the baby looks like me or Seth.

That sudden pain is a fast blow to my gut. I force it down and away though.

"That is the skull, we have a skull forming." I'm grateful for the distraction in Bethany's observation. I don't want anything to steal this moment from me. *I'm having a baby.* This is a happy time. I want my baby to know I'm so happy to see him or her. All I want this baby to feel is loved. Regardless of how fucked up I am.

"There are each of the sections of the skull…" Bethany's professional tone catches me off guard until I realize why she said it.

"Okay, so how far? How far along when the skull forms?"

"I don't… wait, let me…" Bethany doesn't refer to the textbook but instead continues to scrutinize the screen. "There's no yolk sac so you're more than ten weeks along." She's just rattling off facts.

But that's a fact that hits home.

Ten weeks. There's a dull thud in my chest. That confirms it. Seth hasn't been back in my life that long. Plain and simple. I was pregnant when I got in that car with

Laura and saw him for the first time in years. I was already pregnant.

Even though it kills a piece of me, the piece that let him hold me in the living room, pretending we were a happy, perfect couple, I stare at the monitor and force myself not to feel the pain from knowing this isn't Seth's baby. *My baby is okay.*

"Do you want to know if it's a boy or a girl?" Bethany asks, quickly moving the wand from wherever it was positioned so I can't see for myself. As if I could tell what's going on down there. The rotation I did for maternity went by in a blur and the only thing I learned is that I didn't want to work in maternity.

With a quick sniffle to shake any bad or negative energy away, I nod and say, "Yes. Yes, I want to know."

She moves the wand just slightly to the right and the picture on the screen changes. At first I see a little foot, the tiniest little foot and all five toes. Then a leg, followed by both legs and a lean tummy.

"See that?" she asks and I shake my head but don't respond verbally. I'm still in awe that there's a baby in me.

"Boy," she says softly and gently.

"Are you sure?" I question her and then the pain hits again. *Seth wanted a boy.*

"I'm positive," Bethany answers and I smile. Genuinely.

"I'm having a baby boy."

I'm overwhelmed with so many emotions. There's a calmness in seeing my baby boy and knowing he's there and from what I can tell, healthy. But I don't know how Seth will react and that discomfort, that anxiousness, that fear of losing him—it all lingers over the small bit of happiness, tainting it.

"There's hardly any fat."

"What?" I question Bethany's comment.

"That's in the book. It's in here." The excitement from Bethany isn't contagious. Maybe we'll be able to tell how far along we are. There I go again, my mind picturing Seth with me through all of this… "Hold this."

I obey Bethany and hold the wand as still as can be over my belly.

The second I take it, my little boy touches his face. I saw it and I can see each little finger as he does it. My heart swells with the kind of happiness that also makes it ache.

"Did you see?" I whisper the question but Bethany didn't see. That little movement was just for me.

Bethany talks to herself, turning over a page then turning it back again instead of answering. I don't blame her. I hope she's close to knowing.

"He's a little shy of a foot long." Her exhale is loud before she tells me, "I think you're around twenty-two or twenty-three weeks. Definitely not twenty-five weeks because he's not tall enough." She sounds so certain.

"What if he's just short?" I ask her, remembering how my grandma used to tell me how small I was as a baby. I was a teeny tiny preemie.

"Umm, I don't… there's also… I don't know for sure but there's not a lot of fat on him like in these pictures and that's around twenty-five weeks."

"So more than twenty-two but less than twenty-five."

So somewhere around June. I have to take my phone out to double-check. But it would have been a date in June. I can't even begin to think back that far, but I didn't go on many dates at all this summer and the double-dipping I did was in April or May. That's what Bethany called my two nights back-to-back with two different men: double-dipping. Technically I was the one dipped, but either way it doesn't matter. I imagine it won't be hard to figure out what fling led to this little blessing.

Then there's the matter of telling the man… and telling Seth.

"Is that something you can live with?" Bethany asks me and it takes a moment for me to understand what she's referring to. Weeks along: twenty-two to twenty-five.

"Yeah." I don't skip a beat before asking her, "When is it safe to deliver?"

"Thirty-seven weeks… some say thirty-eight."

"What if I get that heart in?" The questions tumble out of me.

"You need to see your doctor." Her tone practically scolds me as she takes the wand from me, taking another long look at the baby. My little prince.

"I will tomorrow." I will do everything right starting tomorrow. Every appointment, every pill. Whatever I have to do.

"It's almost five a.m. love, so you will *today*, but probably after a nap."

"Right, I will after a nap. I will *today*."

"How far along did your doctor say you were? Based on the hormones?"

"She said twenty weeks."

"Okay so maybe I'm wrong… but I mean… he's way longer than ten inches."

"Maybe he's just tall then?" I make a joke but it sounds sad.

"Well make up your mind, is this little one going to be short or tall?" Bethany brightens the joke a bit while she cleans the gel off my stomach. "Just go to see your doctor."

"I can do that," I offer, those emotions still coming in waves but now exhaustion weighs them all down.

"I've got it." She balls up the tissues and then flicks off the machine. "I'd print you pictures but I don't know how, so… go see your doctor later today. Promise me."

"I will. I just…"

Bethany grabs my hand, squeezing it until I look her in the eyes. "I'm here for you and for this little blip."

"I know."

"But you have to tell him."

"I know." This time when I tell her that, I practically whisper because I don't want to tell him.

"Do you think he'll be mad?" she asks nervously, although she tries to hide it.

"I think it will devastate him." I swear to God I'll scream if I cry, but that's exactly what I feel like doing.

"What if… no. No, you can't lie to him. I'm a fucking awful person for even thinking that," she says then shakes her head and I let out a small sad laugh.

"I was thinking if it was anywhere near the date, I'd lie. I'm awful too."

"The truth always comes out anyway." She offers me a hand to sit up and I take it.

"Just tell him the truth already, get it out so it stops stressing you out." She emphasizes, "You don't need that stress. Neither does the baby."

"I know. You're right." My head feels light when I sit up and I have to take a moment to steady myself, crinkling the paper under me.

"You hid from him for how long? You can't hide this."

I would say "I know" again, but… well, she gets it.

Bethany questions me, "You think he'll leave you?"

"I don't. I think it's going to hurt him, though. And make him worry about…" I can't even voice it. *Me running.* Because it's what I always do and why would I stay if I'm pregnant with another man's baby?

Bethany guesses my fear. "He'll think you'll leave him?" I can only nod. "Will you?"

"No." My answer is so firm it's nearly ripped from me. "I'll find out who the father is and then he can be a part of his life or not."

"Seth isn't going to like that."

"I know, but that's what's right, isn't it?"

"I think so."

A moment of silence passes, with nothing but the clock ticking in the background. We have to get going, but I can't move yet.

"I don't know how I can look him in the eyes without telling him but I also don't know how I can tell him this."

"Well, you have to tell him and if you think it will be

less stressful for you, you could write it out now and give it to him. You could call him and let him know. So there's distance."

I still can't answer her.

"There are options and you know the less stress right now for you, the better." She puts her hand on my stomach and I smile faintly. "This baby has to cook a bit longer."

"I can't believe I'm pregnant, much less this far along." It's crazy. Life is one crazy journey.

"Well that's probably a blessing. Looks like you got to skip out on the morning sickness and went straight to the honeymoon phase in the second trimester."

"Right, the horny phase. And to think I thought that was all Seth's doing." I have enough humor to roll my eyes. "Although I really haven't been eating. I just thought my stomach was messed up."

"Why don't you just call him? Let me check out, make sure Cindy is here and I'll stay with you," she practically begs me. "I'm here for you. You call him, and I'll be right here by your side. That way this is done."

I manage to get off the table, imagining calling him to tell him. I won't have to see the devastation on his face and it's selfish, but it's also a relief. A slight one, at just the thought of ripping off the Band-Aid, so to speak.

"Is that okay? Do you want to try calling him?"

I can only nod a response.

"Good. We can hide in here," she tells me over the sound of her balling up the paper that was on the exam table. "Just give me a minute to check out and I'll be back."

All the while she's gone, I think about how I'll tell him.

I'm going to start it the way I want to finish it. *I love you more than anything.* My hand instinctively moves to my belly, wondering if that will hold true. I speak out loud, imagining his reaction to every word. "I'm not leaving you, unless you want me to." The third statement comes out stronger than I thought possible, due to the way it fucking kills me.

"I couldn't sleep tonight, because the doctor called after you left and told me something."

I stand there, alone in the room, and I say everything from the news about my heart to how far along I am. When Bethany comes back, I say it all again, crying through most of it. And leave it all on voicemail because Seth doesn't answer.

I'm all right with that. I'll be home soon. At least I said it all.

I might be with him when he listens to it, but at least he'll hear it all.

It doesn't make me feel any better, though. It doesn't help shield me in the least from thinking my world is crumbling apart.

CHAPTER 6

Seth

THE EARLY MORNING SUN PEEKS OUT OVER THE HORIZON as Declan's car drives away, the image of the train station reflected in the rearview getting smaller by the second.

"You going to say anything?" Declan asks with a hint of humor, but the concern drowning in his gaze and the way he keeps glancing at me even though he's driving and the light ahead is green, says otherwise.

My throat is tight and I clear it, but the unsettling feeling is still there. I can't even look him in the eyes.

"I can't." My eyes feel heavy and the strain of it all is weighing me down even more. "He made me an offer, and it involves silence." *That's a lie.*

"An offer for what?" Declan questions and I let my eyes close as my head falls back.

It can't be true. It hurts too much to even think about it. Laura is all right. I want the videos from the projector filling the high walls of the warehouse and everything he showed me, to be made up. Just a cruel trick. It can't be true.

Rubbing at my eyes with my fist to rid them of both the need to sleep and the sight of what Marcus showed me, I try to answer Declan.

"It involves Laura."

I can feel it happening again, just like it did when I was a teen. The feeling of my world slowly falling apart until there's nothing left but pain and anger. It's happening again.

I lie to Declan, staring straight ahead as the light moves more quickly over the skyline and say, "I can't tell you." I give him a bit of the truth though and add, "I don't even know if he's telling the truth."

Marcus never said a damn thing about keeping secrets. But what he wants from me... I can't tell Declan. I can't tell anyone.

"He threatened Laura?" Declan's tone is a mix of pissed and troubled. His grip slips on the wheel and he stares at me instead of the road.

I shake my head, unable to voice anything as the images come back. I don't want it to be true. Swallowing, I prepare to give Declan any bread crumb I can, but that involves speaking about Laura... and I can't. Not until I talk to her.

The vibrating of my phone in my lap spares me the sorry excuse I was going to give Declan.

It's her. It's my Babygirl. The image of her face fills up

the screen as the phone rings and I know I can't answer it. Not here. Not with Declan listening.

I imagine she's upset with me. She woke up and I wasn't there. I told her I would be and I wasn't.

"You going to answer that?" Declan asks, his voice sounding concerned.

Again, I only shake my head. Still holding the phone, unable to let go, but unable to answer just the same.

"What can I do?" he offers and that simple kindness nearly breaks me.

"I don't know yet," I say, finally answering Declan honestly. I've never felt so lost and helpless. "I have to ask Laura something."

I don't know how I'll even get it out of me. The questions and the accusations are caged deep in my chest.

I feel hopeless, but worse than that, like a traitor. Like I don't deserve to live.

It's silent all the while in the car, up until we park and I notice Laura's car is missing.

It only takes a second to go into my texts and read them. Shit, my heart couldn't beat for the second spent thinking she's already gone.

"I can't leave you like this," Declan says, giving me the side of him I know too well. The true friend I have in him.

"I'll be all right," I say, lying to him again and I know it's a lie as I pull the handle of the door, letting the wind whip at me as I climb out of his car.

It's not until I'm inside that I listen to the voicemail and completely break down.

The sick feeling in my stomach that I had before meeting with Marcus is back full force as I stare at the cup of coffee on the end table. The smell of black coffee invades every inch of space as I rest my elbows on my knees and wait. I can't move off the chair in the living room. I can't drink the coffee even to stay awake from this brutal night.

All I can do is sit here and wait for Laura to walk through the door.

I believe everything Marcus said after listening to her message.

Her heart. The baby.

She didn't tell me the timeline though. She kept so much from me.

My head falls into my hands as I do what I've done for the last half hour. I wait for her.

Everything is wrong. It's all wrong. It's not supposed to happen like this.

I shouldn't have to make a deal with the devil to keep her alive. I shouldn't be this helpless and at his mercy. Not over this. Not like this.

I'm supposed to be able to protect her and keep her safe. I have so many regrets. Too many to count.

The churning in my gut intensifies when I hear a car door shut out front.

My heart breaks slowly, but it still beats. I don't know how it's possible to still function when I know damn well that it's shattered.

There are two things that keep me upright. Two things that prevent me from falling to the ground and giving in to the pain like I did eight years ago when I thought I'd lost Laura forever.

1.   She still loves me. She told me she did.

2.   Marcus's deal.

I might hate myself for it, but if Laura gets to live, I'll do it. I will do anything to save her.

My phone moves from my left hand to my right when the doorknob on the front door turns. Anxiousness creeps up my throat and suffocates me.

The small creak of the door opening fills the room and then she's there, my gorgeous girl. It takes everything in me to stay where I am.

She freezes in the doorway, her gaze caught with mine, but the howl of the wind behind her releases us from the moment. The clicking of her boots is all I can hear until she shuts the door, keeping her hand on it and her back to me to speak.

"You got my message?" she asks even though she already knows.

I flip my phone in my hand and do everything I can just to breathe. "Yeah," I answer her. "Come sit here." I give her the command although my voice isn't as strong as I'd like it to be.

The hollowness in my chest seems to grow, the vacant spot filled with agonizing pain.

Laura sniffles at the door, the tip of her nose bright pink but I'm not sure if it's from the cold or from crying. My poor girl.

Her keys fall onto the foyer table and she kicks off her shoes, leaving them there. Taking her time before coming around to the living room, glancing at the black coffee that's probably cold by now and not a sip has been taken.

Her blue eyes are glossy as her bottom lip quivers. "Are you…" she starts to say before pausing as she slowly takes the seat on the sofa catty-corner to me. The crack in her voice keeps her from getting it out.

"Are you…" she tries again to question me about something and fails as I sit up straighter, still on the edge of the chair and waiting for her to get it out.

Her long lashes flutter as a silent sob seems to make her breath stutter. "I love you," she whispers as her expression crumples.

I can't stand her like this. I can't take it. In a quick single motion, I take all of her. One arm slipping under her ass and the other around her back. I'm on the sofa with her in my lap before I can think twice.

She's warm and soft in my arms, so fragile as I hold her.

With her head laying in the crook of my neck I whisper the only thing I'm sure of against the shell of her ear, "I love you too." Holding on to her as tight as I can, I rock her as she tries to stop crying.

I know the feeling. I understand her when she says she hates crying. I wish I hadn't cried either, but I can hold it together for her. When she needs me, I'm so much stronger than I am without her.

"Shhh," I murmur, rocking her back and forth, grateful that I'm able to just hold her finally.

Time passes, and I wish we could fall asleep right here, and wake up to find last night was just a nightmare. A fucking horrible nightmare.

I know better than to pretend though. Bad things happen when we pretend we're all right.

"I want you to tell me everything," I say, speaking calmly and softly.

"Did you listen to it all?" she asks me, her lips brushing against the rough stubble on my neck with her question.

"I did." Three times and nearly a fourth, but I don't tell her that extra information.

She's still in my arms, her chaotic breathing steadying with each deep inhale and exhale.

The sound of her licking her lips steadies me, preparing to do as I ask. Her not running from me… that steadies me even more.

"I need a transplant for my heart and this baby is further along than we've been together."

"Five months," I cut in, very much aware.

"I think so. I'm going to make an appointment tomorrow."

"Good, schedule everything. I want to go with you." I don't give her the option to say no; it's not a question. And thankfully, she doesn't object. I'm on edge wanting to take control but knowing full well that I lack it in the ways that matter most.

"I should have told you everything. I just couldn't. I couldn't look you in the eyes and tell you. And I'm so sorry."

"And the baby?" I don't even know what my question is.

"I didn't know that until you left last night." Her knees dig into the sofa as she leans back, the words spilling from her lips quickly and she finally looks me in the eyes. "I didn't know how far along I was… I'm sorry… I just…"

I kiss her before her voice can hitch again and before fresh tears fall from her wide eyes. Her lips mold to mine, her hands slip around my neck and she holds on to me as tightly as I hold on to her.

The kiss deepens and that's her doing. Her desire and her need make a deadly concoction as they stir to mingle with her sadness. I'd get drunk on that taste every night if I could.

When she breaks our kiss to breathe, her chest brushing against mine, I whisper, "I love you." I'm drowning in the heat between us.

"I love you too."

I have to ask her before I lose the nerve, before the moment is over. I need to know. "And the father? Are you going to tell him?"

She didn't mention him at all in the message. I imagine she's unsure who he is, but I'll damn well know before the sun sets tonight.

"I'm going to tell him when the baby's here."

She holds my gaze, and hers is mixed with uncertainty as she confesses, "I think he deserves to know."

I nod in agreement although that's not at all what I think. I lie to her like I did to Declan and say, "As long as you want me there at your side, then the world can throw whatever it wants at us, because I know it'll be all right." I don't know if anything is going to be all right. All I know is that I made a deal with the devil and I pray he keeps his word. All I can do is pray and I hate it.

I can hold her all the while though. Every moment I can love her, I will. Her message was very clear about the condition of her heart although she neglected to mention that she'll likely die within the year and that if she doesn't get a donor transplant, she most certainly will.

"Go the bedroom and get undressed," I command her, again not giving her a choice. And again, she's agreeable, kissing me hurriedly as if afraid I'll change my mind and then she slips off my lap.

I miss her warmth instantly, but she has to go without me. I need a moment. Just one to forward the message to Declan and then text him to listen to it.

And then I listen to her again.

I'll need his help to find out who the father is. I add in a message, that Marcus knew. That this is what Marcus told me, which isn't a lie, but Marcus told me much more.

The floor creaks and that's when I see Laura's come back.

"Are you okay?" Laura whispers, drawing my gaze to hers as she stands in front of me, her legs between my knees. I nod into the palm of her hand when she cups my chin.

"I just need a minute, Babygirl." She rewards my whispered response with a kiss and I tell her to go. That I'll just be a minute.

Hate is so much easier to hold on to than any other emotion. And that's all I can think as she leaves me.

She's mine, not his.

This baby is mine, not his.

I text Declan as I listen to Laura's feet pad softly down the hallway: *Find out who Laura dated five months ago. Go through her texts, her emails, the dating apps on her phone. I want to know everything about him.*

CHAPTER 7

Laura

I LOVE HIM WITH ALL MY HEART.

Every piece of it beats for him.

My hands tremble as I undress, taking more time than it should and I know that, but I can't stop picturing him there, his shirt unbuttoned at the collar, his broad shoulders hunched over with a dejected look on his face.

I'll never unsee that look in his eyes, like he was questioning if he still had me, if I was still his, and desperately needed to know.

Because he wants me still. He loves me still.

And I've never needed to feel that more than I need it now.

The door behind me creaks open just as I unhook my bra. It hits the floor just as I spin to face him and before I can move or speak, he's almost on me, closing the distance between us in three broad steps.

His strong arms wrap around me as he gathers me up, capturing my squeal of surprise with his lips in a kiss. I can't hold him close enough as my arms wrap around his broad shoulders. They only stay there for a fraction of a second before I tear at his shirt, needing it off and desperately needing his skin against mine.

I've never felt so close to him, yet so far apart at the same time.

I need more of him and all of him. I want him to surround me and consume me until I am nothing but his. Protected and loved and cherished.

My kisses devour his, but somehow he does just the same to me.

Although it all feels reckless and desperate, he lowers me to the bed as if he has full control. Of course he does; he is so much stronger than I am.

The thought reminds me to tear at his clothes, a button popping off as I do and neither of us care.

In a single motion, Seth parts from my embrace, removing his shirt with one hand over his head and tossing it somewhere behind me.

"On your back," he groans, the depth of his dark gaze stirring with a fire that burns me, singeing my core.

I watch the cords of his muscles tense as he removes his clothes, and then he crawls up the bed to where I'm lying. He slowly inches up my naked body, kissing and nibbling which sends both a chill and a thrilling wave of heat to descend over my body. He takes his time, teasing me while my nails dig into the sheets, desperately holding on to patience. I want him now. To say I'm in need would be a profound understatement.

I suck in a breath before his lips press against mine and in that same moment, he enters me. A swift motion that brings about a stinging pain just as much as it brings an all-consuming pleasure.

His pace is set before I can breathe. His grip on my hips, pinning me in place.

He only stops kissing me to moan in the crook of my neck, "I need to get lost in you." And with his deep voice and rough cadence, raw with need, I feel myself clench around him. Already the heat of the act dances along my skin, from the tips of my toes all the way up my body.

My blunt nails dig into his back, not piercing his skin, but holding on to him for dear life as he rocks himself in me all the way to the hilt.

It's all too much, but that's the only way Seth ever is. Too much, all-consuming. It's the only way he's ever been and I've never been so grateful.

As the pleasure builds inside of me, I stare in the reflection of the dresser mirror, watching his powerful frame as he moves in deep, controlled strokes.

He's a sex god, a man I was never supposed to have. And he takes me with a force and a need that's undeniable. He may be getting lost in me, but I've forever been lost in him. And that's all I want. I would happily roam the earth for all eternity not knowing a damn thing other than what it feels like to be loved by him.

As his pace quickens and my climax gets closer and closer, I pull my eyes away from our reflection, my neck arching with a need to pull away from the intense feelings.

"Don't," Seth scolds me, forcing me to keep my eyes open and stare into his gaze. "Don't stop watching now," he says in a single breath that sounds too easy compared to the cold sweat growing along every inch of my skin. He groans, the sound deep and sexy as he props up my left leg so he can enter me even deeper. "This is my favorite part."

With that confession, he pounds into me. His hips piston and a scream tears through me. The pleasure blazes up my body as I cum, but he doesn't stop. He fucks me harder and more ruthlessly, our reflection only adding to the intensity of the scene before us.

I scream out every time I cum on his cock and he rewards me with nips and sucking along my neck.

He fucks me like he owns me. He makes love to me like I've always been his.

And I love both ways I get to have him, because I love all of him.

When we're both breathless and spent, my body weak from his touch and my heart soothed from him whispering he loves me as he leaves kisses on my neck, he lays beside me, his arm protectively draped over my body.

With my back to his chest, I stare at us in the mirror, loving how we fit together so perfectly, but feeling the pain of uncertainty sneak in between us.

There's so much I don't know about how we'll get through this.

"Everything's going to be okay, right?" I whisper even though I know there's no way for him to know. Somehow, I convince myself that he could know. He could make it all right if he wanted to. Because he's Seth King and he has always ruled my world, my thoughts. He is my fate.

"Of course it is, Babygirl," he answers me and kisses my neck before telling me to sleep. His voice doesn't have the confidence I hoped for. I snuggle closer to him and tell him, "I love you," thinking that I need to make sure I tell him every day, just in case it's our last day together.

"I love you too," he says and his answer soothes me, threatening to lure me to sleep with a wonderful dream. But a truth I've known for far too long keeps my tired eyes open, staring at his in the mirror.

If only love was enough to make all this all right...

CHAPTER 8

Seth

I FEEL FUCKING SICK. LIKE THAT KIND OF ICE-COLD tingle that travels along your skin, but your face is burning up type of sick. I hope I vomit on his cheap knockoff shoes.

That's what this prick is. A knockoff. He's no one.

He's no one echoes in my head as I stare back at him, watching the sweat bead on his neck.

"So you own this place?" Declan asks Jim. Jim Howard. This spineless prick sitting in front of me knocked up Laura.

Squirming in his seat, he puts a false smile on his face. He knows who Declan is, he recognizes our names. He's a pussy, a limp dick. God I hate this bastard. I hate him with everything in me.

I hate the color palette of this rinky-dink shop. Home Brew Coffee looks like every other coffee shop that exists. Except there are rows of bagged ground coffee lined up on shelves to buy. There's a bell above the door. Generic paintings of coffeepots on off-white walls. And red metal chairs around six small tables. Like the one we're sitting at right now.

He clears his throat and starts to say, "Actually," but the one word cracks. He's nervous, jittery, and Declan leans forward, calmly telling him to relax. His crisp suit, fresh shave and charming features make this douche look even more like a pile of shit.

How did she even find him all the way out here? It's hours away. Oh, right, that was his doing. To keep her at a distance and every other hookup he has.

I wish I could reach across the table and smash his face in.

His smile turns more firm and he nods as he says, "Actually, I own it with my wife."

That right there. That hot prick of nausea comes back to me. That's why I hate him like I do.

"Your wife?" I question him, keeping my voice as even as I can although my grip on the glass of ice water tightens to the point that it's strained. Everything is so fucking hot as I sit across from this sorry excuse for a man.

He only nods. It's all he can do.

He can lie on his dating profiles. Give a half-real name with a barren social media profile he made up. And cheat around on his wife while texting his friends about it so they'll cover for him.

"That's right," Declan says and nods, speaking before the man can do anything but glance at me and then back to Declan. "I did see that on the lease."

A full background check and hacking into his phone took less than two hours.

"She's pregnant, right?" I question him, my throat so tight I'm getting light-headed.

Every document Declan handed me this morning I wanted to tear up and shred. I haven't felt pure rage like this in a long damn time.

How could she have been with him? My Babygirl with *him*?

All loathing aside, he's decent looking, though there's nothing remarkable about him. Physically he's more built than average, with a nice-enough smile and charming way about him. It's the charm that hides the asshole side. I know the type.

He told her he had a business, which he does, but the online coffee sales barely break even every year. Even this small-time coffee shop, where he really makes his money, is failing. What the hell did he say to her that led to the two of them in bed together?

I imagine he lied. Because that's what pricks like him do. They lie.

The mental image of Jim and my girl is what I see when the bastard responds, "He was just born. Nine pounds and healthy."

"Congratulations," Declan tells him, his smile nice and even. It relaxes the man, and I watch as the tension in his shoulders visible lessens. Like he's genuinely happy he had a son.

I don't expect the other emotions to creep in. The jealousy, the pain and agony. It makes everything in me tense and tight.

He had a wife, he had a baby coming. And he risked losing it all for a "fuck night," as he referred to it in a group message to his friends.

Fuck him.

I swallow down the unwanted emotions with a gulp of water.

"See, I was just wondering," Declan says and his tone changes, lowering as he hunches forward. It takes everything in me to just sit here. Simple as that. Just to stay seated, I am at the edge of my sanity.

His cock was inside her. Did she even get off?

I can't stop fucking wondering. Pissed off and brokenhearted is a strange combination. Jealousy disgusts me. And yet here I am, jealous of this piece of shit.

"Your profile, the one you've been using to see some of the women around here, it says you're single."

I can hear the prick swallow, the sound giving me slight relief. I want to see him choke on his fear.

If Laura knew, she'd hate herself. She'd blame herself for sleeping with a married man. I know she would.

"If I…" Jim pauses and throws his hands up in a defensive gesture as if he's being robbed and I turn to my left, just enough to see the young woman at the register pausing as she cleans the glass coffee mugs.

"Maybe you should go to the back, sweetheart," I tell her and give her the hint of a smile that narrows my eyes. When she glances between me and Jim, I add, "Nothing to worry about. Just asking questions."

I surprise myself by how easy it all comes out. I don't feel a hint of that ease inside of me.

The conversation pauses as the woman leaves the main room, hesitating at the doorway to the storage room.

"We'll only be a minute, promise," Declan reassures her although she doesn't take her eyes off of her employer, whose eyes are pleading.

"Look man, if I slept with someone I shouldn't have, I swear I didn't know." His plea tumbles out followed by heavier breathing.

"Relax." Declan keeps talking, giving him a false sense of reassurance. "We're just confused. We want to know what kind of guy you are because we're moving a little closer and wanted to get the lay of the land is all. You're not in any trouble with us," Declan says and motions with his thumb for emphasis.

The fuck he isn't. I keep my thoughts to myself, though. I'm still not able to speak.

"So you're a married man with a baby."

"Three kids now. Two are in school and we decided to do it all again."

Three of them. I can't stand this man, so how could I be jealous of him? I hate him. I hate everything about him.

The clock on the far wall ticks steadily with every second that passes and I have to stare at it instead of him.

"But you get some side action," Declan questions easily.

My thumb moves in a steady motion across the beads of water on the outside of the glass.

"Yeah," Jim says and leans back, breathing out. "It's just a release."

Crack. The glass in my hand breaks out of nowhere. I only gripped it for a fraction of a second. The glass lays in pieces on the table, the water splashing.

Adrenaline races through me.

Just a release. Laura was "just a release."

"Sorry about that," Declan says and I can barely hear it over the ringing in my ears.

Just a release.

"My friend has a strong grip."

My gaze falls to the prick who just referred to my Babygirl as "a release" when he speaks. "I can see that." The nervousness is back, the jitteriness is evident.

Declan places a hand on my forearm that's under the table, keeping it down. With my free hand I make a fist and lay it on the table, not bothering to clean up the small bit of blood that's there.

If I move, I know exactly what I'll do.

I'll lay into him. I envision it as Declan and he make small talk. I picture slamming my fist against his mouth. The mouth that got to kiss her. He was able to be with her and that's what he refers to it as? *A release.*

Every time he looks at me, I hope he can see what I want to do to him. Judging by the way he averts his eyes the moment our gazes meet and how he turns paler and paler, I think he knows.

"Give us a minute, will you?" Declan asks him kindly. He sounds so friendly, but even with all that ease he gives to the man across from us, Declan grips my forearm harder, silently letting me know what I'm feeling.

It fucking hurts. It feels like my chest is cracked wide open and this bastard did it.

The second the man is behind the counter, I storm out of there, shoving the door open. The harsh wind and bitter cold greet me, chilling me to the bone and I'm thankful for it.

Thankful for anything to dull this pain and this heat that's suffocating me.

"A release," I finally speak as we get to the car. My muscles are bunched, my nostrils flaring when I get in the car, barely taking anything in as my vision goes red.

My voice trembles when Declan takes his seat, the driver's seat. "A release. That's what she was to him!"

I can't control my temper or the way my chest heaves.

"First, don't fuck up my car," Declan says and I whip around to face him. A humorous smirk is waiting there for me.

It dulls the edge of it all, but only just slightly.

When I fall back into the seat, a hand over my eyes, my palm pressing slightly to try to calm myself down, he adds, "He's a prick. He's a liar. But you have to think, what did he mean to her?"

"She was 'a release' to him," I say dully, swallowing the bitter pill before looking at Declan.

"And what was *he* to *her*?" Declan repeats, carefully with emphasis, and his hand lands on my shoulder in a way that's meant to calm me, to get through to me.

But all I can see is that bastard fucking my girl.

"She's going to have his baby." The words choke me as I say them.

"You know how it is. Laura's a smart girl; she never messaged him again. He was just a release for her too."

My voice raises, the anger showing with a spiteful tone, "Well all that's changed now, hasn't it?"

It's silent, apart from the sound of the wind howling so loud and commanding outside that it rocks the car. I rub my hand down my face, trying to rid myself of the need to do something about what he did to her. How he lied to her and used her.

"I want to go back in there and beat him to death," I confess to Declan although I stare down at my shoes, the black leather impeccably polished and shined. They're expensive as fuck, but they feel like nothing. I feel like I'm not worth a damn thing compared to that prick.

Just the sight of him makes me feel like I'm nothing. Because it's his baby. He has what I so desperately want. If he wanted, he could have a family with her.

"I hate him too," Declan finally answers me, his hand patting my back as I stay hunched over in the car. "You want to kill him… fuck him up? Whatever you want, I'm here for you."

I nod. Yes, that's exactly what I want.

"But think for a moment about what he was to her," he implores me. "He doesn't mean anything to her."

"He gets to be the father of her baby." The second I speak the words, I hate them. I want to take them back and do everything I can to keep that reality from happening.

He got his release, so as far as I'm concerned, he doesn't get to have anything else. Anger is blinding me to reason.

"Block him everywhere and erase it all." I give the command to Declan and add, "She won't be able to find him. Their only contact was through that dating app. He's the only one she slept with that month, so she'll know it was him when she looks at her schedule. Block him everywhere. Erase him from her life."

As Declan takes in a slow breath, his expression falls. He doesn't agree with my decision. I can see it written on his face.

"He can't be in her life or I'll kill him," I say and wait for Declan to look back at me before I hold his stare. "I will kill him. I know I will."

Pulling his hand back, he scratches the side of his jaw like he's thinking, right before telling me, "Don't take her control away."

My head shakes as I release a huff of a breath. "I'll do it myself then," I say and the words sound spiteful as they come out.

"Seth. Listen to me," he says and his tone begs me. "She wants to do the right thing. She always wants to do the right thing."

"I know." I can't stress it enough. "I know who she is. I know what kind of person she is." I'm pissed and I can't not be pissed because all that's left for me otherwise is the hurt.

Declan keeps his voice low and calm as he says, "I'll make it so she can message him and it'll show as seen but he won't ever see it."

With the ringing in my head it takes me a moment to absorb what he's saying. She can message him, but he won't see it. He'll never know. He won't be able to respond. It's what he fucking deserves. "Can you do that?"

Declan nods as a car drives by us and that's when reality sneaks back in. It's fucking cold and we're having a therapy session on the side of the road in a parked car.

"I can," he tells me and I sit up straighter, clearing my throat and focusing on getting my shit together.

"He'll be out of the picture then," I comment, feeling lighter and more relieved than I imagined I would. There's still her heart to worry about, but one problem solved makes all of this feel like it could work. I can keep her and my baby.

She'll still love me. She won't leave me.

But then that leaves me with Marcus's deal.

"I'm getting my guys on it now," Declan says although it's a question more than anything.

"Yeah," I answer him and then clear my throat. "Yeah, thanks man."

I picture her staring at the screen and not getting a response and it fucking kills me because I know it will hurt her. "She's going to be wrecked by it."

"She just wants to do the right thing," Declan says, disagreeing with me. He doesn't know how emotional she is, though. She's strong and smart, but emotions rule her every thought and action. "She can do that. She can message him still." Even though he's talking to me, he's texting. Sending out demands for all this bullshit.

I'm barely hanging on, the anger's got nowhere to go and all I am is fucking wrecked.

My voice is tight and my words crack when I tell Declan, "I waited too long."

The truth hurts. It's brutal and unforgiving. More than that though, it's deserved.

"What?" he says then looks up and at me. His eyes on me beg me to look at him, but I don't. I can't. There's a prick in the back of my eyes and I feel like a little bitch. Licking my lips, I take in a deep breath, expecting that to make it better, but it's worse.

"He's what she had. A release is all she had." I barely get the words out and I ignore Declan when he reaches out to comfort me.

"I could have been there with her. I was so close for so long and I could have been with her."

"Hey, man, don't—"

"She's dying and that's what she had," I say, cutting him off as tears cloud my vision. She's dying.

I can fix this problem named Jim Howard, though. I can get rid of the man who didn't love her but has a rightful place in her life. I won't allow that. I can't.

This baby is mine and so is she.

But I can't fix her heart. I can't fix that; I'm so damn helpless.

"I waited too long."

Marcus's promise, his deal, whispers darkly in the back of my mind. He swears he can save her. He promised. He's willing to make that deal.

Declan's still trying to console me when I say, "I have to tell you something."

Fate's a bitch though, choosing this exact second to make his phone ring in his hand.

Pulling me from the moment.

"Get it," I tell him and then stare at the window, pretending like everything isn't still crumbling around me. "This can wait."

It can't.

None of it can wait.

Marcus will want his answer soon. And time isn't on Laura's side.

CHAPTER 9

Laura

"**S**O GOOD NEWS AND BAD NEWS," I START TO TELL Bethany. The hot chocolate on the table smells divine and with how tired I am, I'm going to need another one in no more than thirty minutes after I suck this one down just to stay awake for this shift.

In the last ten days, I've had every test done and every checkup imaginable. The days have blurred to the point where all I can see is Doctor Tabor's face during the day and Seth's at night.

"Spill it." With her coffee in hand she stares at me, waiting expectantly. She'd look very commanding and badass if it wasn't for the puppy dogs on her pale blue scrubs.

"So the good news," I say and pull out the slippery

paper with the black-and-white image on it. The one with my baby boy's perfect little face as he sucks his little thumb.

My insides turn to warm goo every time I look at him. "He's perfect," I tell her and the smile on my face is infectious.

"And beautiful," Bethany adds, taking the paper and staring at it.

It's quiet for a moment as we both pretend we're not emotional wrecks still. We don't talk about my heart and when I feel it racing, I just keep it a secret. I don't want them to worry, but both Bethany and Seth tiptoe around me whenever I go quiet. It is what it is. A baby will really throw a wrench into being a hard-ass like I used to see myself. So instead of telling them that my heart feels like it wants out of my chest, I tell them I thought the baby was kicking. That always makes them smile. I would so much rather them smile and celebrate with me, than be scared … like I am. I'm so damn scared I can barely function.

I have to tell someone though and Bethany is the someone who can handle this.

"What's the bad news?" Bethany asks, handing me back the photograph and opting to hold her coffee with both hands.

"That copy's yours," I tell her and force a smile but it wavers. Clearing my throat and staring at the large clock to the right of the elevators, I tell her, "Because I won't accept a donor organ or surgery until it's safe for the baby, my placement has dropped on this list." The air leaves my lungs and said heart does a quick race, pounding against my rib cage. It does it every time I think about it, but I'm quick to look down at the picture. "I accept it," I tell both of them. Both Bethany and my little one. "I accept waiting to make sure this little one makes it out healthy."

There's no response but I can feel her gaze on me. It's too damn quiet this late at night. The ticking from the clock is all I get so I pick up the cup of cocoa to have a drink, only to find it already empty. I must've sucked it down without realizing. It makes a hollow sound when I set it down on the front desk.

"I've thought a lot about it, Bethany. I choose the baby. Please don't ask me not to." I have to whisper the last statement. I know that's what Seth would do. Seth would want the heart as soon as possible. He wouldn't risk another day. But this baby isn't ready and I don't want to live if it's at the expense of my child. I want to give this baby everything and I choose to start right now with these days, however many of them I can give him.

"What did the doctor say?" she asks.

"She said it's not wise." As I speak, I mimic the way the doctor said it. As if I was supposed to answer with absolutely no emotion and only logic. "My heart does more work as the pregnancy progresses. She said that's probably why my symptoms have been worse recently."

"That worries me," she says and Bethany's response is quiet, smothered with concern and I wish I could allay her fears, but she's right. It's a risk and a very real one at that.

"We're going to plan for a C-section roughly sixteen weeks from now, and the baby is already getting steroid shots for his lungs and other organs to develop. With the C-section there will be far less stress on my heart, so there's that positive."

I try to keep my response upbeat, but Bethany doesn't buy it.

She's silent and it takes me a long moment to bring myself to look at her, but she's staring down at the slip of thermal recording paper from the ultrasound in my hand. She wipes away the tears in her eyes when she sees me looking at her.

"Right. And then when he's born, what happens as far as the surgery for your heart?"

"Top of the list."

"Okay…" She seems hesitant although my answer was quick and confident. "And what happens in the meantime?"

"Vitamins, medication and appointments … baby yoga and a less stressful schedule. Which means …" I pause to suck in a breath and then reluctantly let it out. "I'm trying to decide if I should take leave. I don't have to be on bed rest, I specifically asked… but my doctor did recommend taking a leave of absence so I could eliminate as much stress as possible."

"You should," she says and Bethany's response is immediate and adamant. "Go home. Stay home."

"Part of me wants to … but the bigger part of me doesn't. I want to be here where I'm needed … It's not like Seth can just up and quit. You know how it is. So I'd just be home alone. Worrying constantly … I'd rather worry about everyone else in this place than think about myself for even a minute."

"Do you really want to be on your deathbed wishing you worked more?"

I shrug, even though I know the answer to that. I've thought so much about it these past few days.

If I'm on my deathbed, I know exactly what I'll regret.

Every milestone I didn't have with Seth.

I have this horrible feeling that we won't make it to any more of them. It's okay. I just want him to love me and he does. That is enough. It's more than enough for now.

With only that shrug from me, Bethany lets out an exasperated sigh.

"Don't you think Seth would want to be with you right now?" I pick at the sleeve of my scrubs where the fabric is worn as the heat kicks on and a visitor gives us a small wave as she signs in. If only they knew what we were talking about. I glance at the clipboard on the table, knowing I need to sort meds soon, rather than answer Bethany. "What did he say about all of this?"

I rub my tired eyes with the sleeve of my old white scrubs. Mascara mars the pretty fabric. *Sweetie,* which is written all over the scrubs and mixed in with the pattern of peaches, is unrecognizable on my sleeve now.

With my lack of a response, Bethany questions me again, her tone more confrontational. "What did Seth say?"

Looking her dead in the eyes, I answer, "I'm not telling him."

Fuck, it hurts. My throat goes tight at the thought of

keeping this from him. He told me he wants to know everything, but I can't tell him this. I can't do it.

Her wide eyes swirl with disappointment.

"He doesn't need that stress. I want him to think everything is as good as it can be. And it is. I'm doing the best I can and I just want him to be happy with me." I swallow my conviction. "I want him to be by my side but not running my life right now."

I'm prepared for Bethany to be the other half of the argument that I've had in the back of my mind every night as I lie down with him in bed.

He holds me tight, his hand splayed across my belly.

"He keeps calling him 'our little prince.'" My eyes tear up and I have to close them, the watery vision of the silver doors to the elevator turning black and instead I see him. I see the love of my life holding me, talking about my son as if he's his and everything is going to be okay. "I love that he is being the father figure and…" I have to pause when emotions tackle the words as they climb up my throat.

"If I choose this baby over me and he knows… I'm afraid he won't feel the same way. The baby won't be his little prince anymore if something happens to me."

The warm tears come and go now. I'm so used to them I don't fight them.

"Laura." Bethany's pained voice forces me to open my eyes and all I can see is her leaning closer to me, holding me as she shushes me and tells me it's going to be all right.

It's what we do. We say it'll be all right even when we don't know it will.

I love Seth and he loves me. But if I die and this baby lives, I want him to love the baby like he does now. To hold this baby the way he holds me at night.

I don't want to risk him blaming the baby.

"You know my mom left… she blamed me. My mom and dad split because of me. It's what people said anyway."

"Your mom was a bitch and you are not. She was selfish." Bethany knows all about it. We've shared our stories with each other on drunken Wine Down Wednesdays. My mother and her father… what a pair they would have made.

"I might never get a heart but if this baby has Seth, all of him with how hard and fiercely he loves… it'll be okay. And you, of course. His godmother." I deliberately pull away and change the topic as quickly as I can.

"His godmother?" Bethany plays along, ignoring the worry, sticking with the "it's going to be okay" strategy. I want to pretend too. We can all pretend together.

"Yes, if you would be his godmother, I would be so happy."

"Of course." Her nod is furious and her voice sounds ecstatic although the worry still dances in her gaze that's glued to mine.

"Well that's settled then," I say and nod, trying to forget the last bit of our conversation, one of the many worries that keeps me up at night.

With a hand on my belly, on top of a very clear but small bump, I rub my thumb in soothing circles.

My baby will be all right.

I'll get a heart.

Seth will love both of us forever.

We're going to be a family.

Even as I list the positives to counter every doubt I have, I know it's too good to be true.

"Hey," Bethany says and whispers my name, "I know life hasn't been the best to you, but you do deserve your happily ever after."

My hand trembles a bit as I reach for the cup of cocoa, only to find it empty—again. A huff of sarcasm leaves me as I smack it down on the tabletop.

I struggle to respond, not knowing how to tell her one of the greatest truths in life: *not everyone gets a happily ever after.* It's not about what people deserve. Sometimes fate just takes what she wants and there's no rhyme or reason to it.

CHAPTER 10

Seth

"**Y**OUR STOMACH BOTHERING YOU?" I QUESTION Laura at the sound of her fork scraping against the porcelain. "You've barely eaten."

The dining room is something I've barely ever used since moving in here. Tonight's the first night we've used it together. That'll change when the baby comes. A lot of things are going to change.

She leans forward, an elbow resting on the walnut table and glances down at the Chinese food on her plate. It's her favorite, and she still hasn't eaten. She barely eats; she barely sleeps.

With bags under her eyes, she gives me the smallest of smiles. "I think if I eat it, I may in fact throw up."

"What about the lemons?" I offer, changing the subject

and shoving the last wonton into my mouth. She has supplements to help her retain whatever nutrients and fats she can eat because she hasn't gained enough weight. I don't think it's the pregnancy at all. It's the stress. I'm guilty as fuck when it comes to that.

"Oh my God, if I smell another lemon." She breathes out the statement in one long line. "Maybe it works for some women but not me. I'm just not hungry. It's not like I'm nauseated. I'm just not hungry and if I try to eat, that's when my stomach gets upset. There's no morning sickness... I just can't eat."

"What about something else? Anything else?" I offer.

"Let's just lie down on the sofa and relax?" she questions and I'm already standing, the feet of the chair scraping against the hardwood floor making the only noise in the room. "Maybe I'll grab a bowl of ice cream after. A bowl late at night has been wonderful."

"I'll get the dishes," I offer. "Go lie down and put something on the TV."

The light from the black iron chandelier above the table reflects off her hair as she stands up. It gives her the look of an angel.

"I can get it. I'm not useless, you know?" she answers with a simper and the glint in her eye turns soft and tempting.

The gray walls and sleek slate-colored chairs with expensive fabric look cheap compared to the way Laura looks right now, standing there in a simple silk chemise.

"Get your ass on that sofa." To say it's a demand would

be comical, but she obeys, giving me a view and when she turns, I get a good look at her little bump.

The click and light of the TV turning on are followed by dull sounds of channels flicking and by the time I've cleaned up and made my way to her, she's nestled under the chenille throw, a pillow propping up her head as she lies on the end of the sofa, leaving me room behind her to spoon.

Just how she likes it. Which happens to be how I love it.

Just the sight of her like that, knowing she's all mine right now, makes me eager to feel her body pressed against mine.

I'll never not want her. There isn't a day in this life that I wouldn't be drawn to this woman.

She peeks up at me as I slip behind her on the sofa. All of her soft curves molding to mine and warming every inch of me.

As she snuggles against me, she holds up the remote to the TV, flicking through the channels without actually waiting to see what's on the screen.

"What are we watching?" I ask her, sneaking a small kiss on the crook of her neck. Her eyes close and the corners of her lips slip up. I love it. I love the way she reacts to something so small.

The moment she opens them, she shrugs and sets the remote down, leaving the TV to play an old cartoon although the volume is so low, I can barely hear it.

"You're going to be a good dad, you know that?"

She picks nervously at the end of the throw and I don't answer her until she looks back at me. "You will be."

If only.

"You'll tell me if I do something wrong, won't you?" I play it up, wanting her to be happy, needing her not to have a worry in the world other than what flavor of ice cream she wants tonight.

"I would say that you won't do anything wrong... but you totally will." Her brutal honesty does nothing but make me smile, which in turn puts a grin on her face and I swear it's the first time everything has seemed right all day. That sick feeling inside that haunts me, warning me that nothing is all right is silenced by the way she looks at me.

Pulling her body close to mine, my forearm against her front and her back against my chest, I live in this very small moment for as long as I can.

When I kiss the crown of her head, she hums a sweet sound, my favorite sound.

"I wanted to talk to you about a few things," Laura says just beneath her breath and then gently turns in my arms. I have to loosen my grip some for her to get settled right.

"What about?" I ask her, knowing damn well whatever she's going to bring up, she's been thinking about for days.

"I think I may quit... or go part-time." She stares at the dip in my throat as she talks. As I answer her, she rests her pointer against it before dragging it up my neck and back down. I stare at her all the while, from the curve of her neck to the tip of her nose. How every feature of her is utterly gorgeous.

"You never have to work if you don't want to."

"I don't know what's best to do."

"Whatever you want to do, I will be here. I will support you. And I will love you regardless of your choice." That's what I tell myself every night. To love her, to stay with her. Because it's all I want back from her. If that happens, we'll be okay.

When all of this is over, we have to be okay. That's the bottom line. I won't survive if we aren't together.

Or if she doesn't love me anymore. So I'm careful. Careful not to do anything that will push her away.

"I mean it," I tell her adamantly, waiting for her gaze to meet mine. "Whatever you want to do."

"Thank you," she whispers and then her breath hitches. The next question is muffled as it comes out, like it didn't want to be asked. "Can I ask you something?" She's quick to follow it up with, "I don't want to upset you."

As she clears her throat, looking down at my chest again rather than into my eyes, I nod and say, "Of course, ask me anything."

All of the innocuous questions she could have possibly asked are nothing like the one she utters.

"Did my dad die quick?"

I'm gutted by her question. I can't speak for a second, I can't do anything but stare down at her as she tries not to cry.

Her inhales are deliberate and even as she says, "I just wanted to know. I've been thinking about him a lot, you know?"

The memory of him on his knees in front of me is a flash in my eyes and I'm grateful she doesn't look at them for fear the reflection in them would give it away.

"It was fast," I answer her as evenly as I can. "I'm sorry."

"Just a shot to his head?" she questions further and it fucking kills me. "Did he know?"

"He knew. When he got there, he knew." I don't know how she can lie here with me during this conversation. It makes me feel like that much more of a bastard.

"Right and then it was fast." She keeps picking at the blanket, staring at my chest as her shoulders move gently up and down with her even breathing.

"It was. He wasn't greedy. He was..."

"He was stupid," she answers for me, with no resentment or emotion. Just simply matter-of-fact. "He never should have been a part of that life."

I want to agree with her, but I'm afraid to speak at all on it. It's not my place.

"He used to tell me all sorts of things he shouldn't."

I'm grateful she hasn't pulled away. I'm thankful she doesn't break down either. But damn does it hurt. "If I could go back and..."

She peers up at me, her eyes darker, wider, swirling with a knowing truth as she says, "It wouldn't have changed it, would it?"

With my throat tight, I shake my head and hold on to her tighter.

"He just didn't think it through. His mouth would

move before his brain. Grandma said it too. She worried for him because he couldn't keep his mouth shut."

"I'm sorry." It's all I can say. "That's who my dad was." She keeps talking, although it's as if she's talking to herself rather than me. Her gaze firmly set on my shoulder this time, her finger trailing along the seam of my t-shirt. "A know-it-all who didn't know a damn thing and a man who ran his mouth faster than he himself could run."

"There were good parts to him," I offer her, remembering her father. "I wasn't around him often, but when I was, he loved to make jokes. He liked for other people to smile."

Her hand pauses and worried, I gaze down at her, only to see a small smile gracing her lips. "That's true. He did like to make other people happy."

"He did." Picking up her hand, I kiss her knuckles.

A long moment passes, the comfortable atmosphere dampened and the irony of childhood cartoons playing in the background only adds to the somber effect.

"Thank you for still loving me." I don't know how I'm able to speak with the way every part of me dies inside. What I did was unforgivable. I stole from her in a way no one had a right to. And yet here she is, letting me hold her and soothe the pain I caused.

"He wasn't the best father, but he loved me."

"He did."

"Promise me, Seth, that you'll love this little boy."

"Our little boy," I correct her and then kiss away the tears on her cheek.

"Yes," she says and smiles through the pain. "Promise me you'll love him always."

I hate the way she's talking right now. Maybe she thinks I don't see through her words. To the very idea that she's planning a life for me and for our little prince without her. I won't let it happen. I can't.

I can't live without her.

"Always. I will love you and our son, and all of the other little ones to come, forever."

"I love you forever," she whispers, tilting up her chin and brushing her lips against mine. It's the way she used to do it. She'd say she loved me, then kiss me, so when I didn't say it back, it was okay. Like she'd silenced me and not as if I was deliberately holding back.

I pull away from her, breaking the tender kiss and stare into her baby blues as I say, "I love you forever and ever, Babygirl."

CHAPTER 11

Laura

I CAN'T HAVE WINE. WHICH IS MY NORMAL GO-TO FOR stress.

And just the thought of carbs makes me want to puke. So my junk food choices are a no go. My mind races whenever I try to nap, even though I'm exhausted as all hell.

So what's a girl to do? Shop.

"We are buying all the things. Every single thing," I state comically as I toss another blue binky into the cart. "I didn't realize they were called pacifiers," I comment as I read the back of another package. This one contains a binky with a little blue airplane on the front and even comes with a strap to hook it onto a onesie so it doesn't get lost. *How smart.*

"What? What did you think they were called?" Bethany questions and I shrug. "I've only ever heard it called a 'binky.'"

She's still busy reading the side of a bottle warmer. It's the third one she's picked up. None of them seem to be good enough and I'm not sure what deems them unacceptable.

"You know you can't get everything on your own. You need to have a shower so we can get you stuff too."

"And who exactly am I going to invite?" I almost say Melody, just to jokingly name a patient, but then the last time I saw her comes back to me, along with a chill that silences me.

"I think…" Bethany starts to answer me but she's distracted by another box, which she picks up to examine then puts down. She pushes the cart down the aisle further and I walk with her, resisting the urge to grab every bath toy on the display wall as we go.

For noon on a Wednesday, the Buy Buy Baby store is practically empty and it's just us two. "You know, I think it would be good if you met the other girls," she says and finally looks at me, standing still with both hands on the handle of the cart.

"Other girls?" I question and she pulls her gray shimmery sweater up her forearms and bunches it just before her elbows. It is a little hot in here, after all.

"You know, Aria, Chloe, Addison."

The wives of the Cross brothers.

"Oh," is all I can answer. I'm shocked, to be honest.

And then a little petrified. I got out of the life. I know Seth comes with it. But this is different. Things are different now. Aren't they? Loneliness and longing are two emotions I didn't expect to feel at that thought. "Is that because you and Jase are… you know, a real thing now. Like for real, for real?"

"For real, for real." Her cheeks get fuller when she smiles. Every time I mention his name, she smiles like that.

"I think you'd really like them and Aria… last night she did a reading for me. And I picked a card for you. She said you're not supposed to and it doesn't work like that. But I think it fit you well."

It takes me a moment to realize by reading she means tarot cards.

"What card?" I ask her even though I turn my attention to a pile of baby blankets. I run my hand along them, but I don't really feel them. Just the thought of the Cross brothers and those women gives me pause. But if they're a part of Seth's world…

"The three of cups. She said it's the card of sisterhood."

I turn to her with a smirk and say, "Sisterhood?" She only nods.

"Look, they would love you and you would love them, and," she stops and sighs like whatever she has to say next is a given before continuing, "if I have to be around them, so do you."

A single laugh comes from deep in my chest and makes me smile.

"Well then—" I start to answer her, but that's when

I feel it. "Oh my gosh," I say as both of my hands fly to my lower belly. Very low, close to my hips. And he does it again.

"What? What is it?" Bethany's voice is riddled with unease until I smile the widest grin I've had in weeks.

"He kicked." I take her wrist as she gapes and gently put her hand right where mine was. I'm careful as I do it, worried he'll stop. The anxiousness keeps me on my toes, holding my breath until Bethany squeals, "He kicked!"

He kicked. My grin stretches all the way across my face. My baby kicked for the first time in a baby supply shop, right at the start of aisle ten. I never want to forget this moment. The smile genuine, the happiness and relief so very real. This is what it's supposed to feel like. It's what normal women must imagine when thinking about being pregnant.

No matter what happens, I got to have this moment. With my best friend hugging me, and my baby safe and healthy. I'll be forever grateful that I at least got to have this moment.

"One cup of coffee, two cups of water." The waitress looks at me like I'm crazy for about half a second before she corrects her maybe-seventeen-year-old face.

I'm tired as all hell and if I need a cup of coffee… well then I need a cup of coffee. My doctor said a cup is fine as long as I drink water constantly and it might help me with other issues I'm having too. The headaches, the lack of being able to go to the bathroom.

The second the waitress, I think she said her name was Angel, turns away from us and moves to the next table, Bethany tells me, "I am taking off for the next one."

"It's on Thursday." Because I'm high risk, I have to go in for stress tests constantly.

"I'm going to miss you at work, so I want to come along."

"I'd love that." With both of my arms folded in front of me and resting on the table, I try to pick an item on the menu that calls out to me. The menu is printed on paper with a checkerboard pattern and the tabletop is red lacquered. It fits the '50s feel of the place.

The linoleum floors and pleather bench seats do too.

There are a lot of yummy smells in the Bells Diner but one thing in particular smells divine. "I'm actually craving something," I mumble and when Bethany asks me what, I can only shrug. "I'm not sure what. But something…"

That gets a laugh from her and although I hate to interrupt the happy day with one little thing, I have to do it. Better now than later.

"I have something to ask you," I say and tap my finger on the menu, no longer searching for my Goldilocks dish, fidgeting with a ring on my middle finger. It's a rose gold ring with a white quartz stone and flowers on the edges of the band… little daisies. Cami gave it to me a long time ago and I rediscovered it last night when I went looking through things as I packed them up to take to Seth's place.

He hates it when I call it that. It's *our* place now. I could roll my eyes at that all day long. I'll make it ours, but right now it's his place with a bunch of my boxes and things in it. Like this ring. An old friendship ring she told me once that was supposed to guard us from bad things. I didn't wear it for the longest time, thinking it had done just the opposite.

"If I die, will you take care of him?"

The thud in my chest is nothing compared to what I feel every night. I won't feel better until he's in my arms. That's simply the way it is. The unknown isn't just uncomfortable, it's scary as fuck. And it's weird between Seth and me without knowing for certain that there's a backup plan. A "just in case" plan. I can't talk about it with him though.

The shock on Bethany's face is temporary. It morphs into something more mortified but then solemn.

The cords in her neck tighten as she averts her gaze but starts to say something.

"Here you go." Angel, our waitress, interrupts us. The cups hit the table one by one, the waters, coffee, and a latte for Bethany, and then she asks us if we need another minute to look over the menu.

"We do, please," I answer her quickly and pray that when she scuttles off that the only thing Bethany will say is, *of course.*

"What about Seth?"

That's the last thing I wanted her to ask.

"I don't know how he'll react if I… he's been very emotional lately. I worry about him." My hand travels to my lower belly, and I wish my little prince would kick again.

"I just need to know that our baby will be all right. I can't imagine… I just can't see him dealing with me not being there and also having a baby dropped in his lap.

"It will be hard for him to keep it together," I explain calmly, rationally. There are no tears when I say it out loud. Because I know it's a true fear of mine. If I die and Seth is left with a helpless baby… If he breaks down, our little boy is going to need someone there.

"I'm just coming to terms with the fact that a heart may never come and I don't know that Seth will be able to take care of him on his own, at least in the beginning." I don't know that I'm describing this right. I've been too busy picking at my nails to realize Bethany is silently crying.

"You aren't allowed to cry. We're in public and we aren't drunk," I mock scold her emotional reaction comically. I hate to see her like this. It hurts a piece of me that's always wounded. The part that knows I can't help that one day, I won't be there for her. For my baby boy. For Seth. One day, I won't have them and they won't have me.

"They're going to need you. I need you there for them. Both of them." This feels like the last piece of the puzzle. Seth doesn't know it, but at least I'll feel more at ease.

"I know that you're just planning." She toys with the fork on the table as she talks. Breathing in deep, she finally looks back at me and says, "I promise if you… if something happens to you," I don't miss how she doesn't say, *if you die*, "then yes, I will make sure your baby boy is safe and happy and lives the best life a little boy could."

"Thank you, Bethany." She nods.

"I'm not ready to die and this life wasn't what I planned, but I want to make sure he'll be all right. Seth too."

"You're going to be okay, though." She sounds far too confident, but at least she's stopped tearing up.

"Sure I will," I answer her with a smirk and have a taste of my far too bitter coffee before reaching for the sugar. That's when I see the long blond hair out of the corner of my eye.

Chills sweep over me and I turn sharply to my left, to the booth where a blonde woman was seated with her back to me.

I only blinked and now she's gone.

She was there, though. She was right there. Fear whips around me, nearly making me knock over the sugar.

"You okay?" Bethany questions. "Hey, love, you all right?"

"Yeah, yeah," I struggle to answer her while also trying to find the blonde woman I know I've seen a handful of times now. I know I saw her.

"Did you take your medication?" she asks softly, her hand over mine.

"What? Yes, yes, of course I did." Even though she's not there, I'm still uneasy and it's hard to shake it off.

No one's there.

"I have a question then. What if Seth doesn't want me involved? That's the only thing I worry about. What if he wants to leave with your son and go back to the West Coast? What if he takes him... what are we calling him? Have you thought of any names?"

I answer, "Little prince."

I can barely focus on her question, still struck with the image of the blonde who reminds me so much of Cami.

Fuck, I really am going crazy.

"Well, what then? What if he leaves?"

"Seth isn't a loner. He doesn't do well alone, so that won't happen." I surprise myself with my quick answer and confidence, but it's true. It's simply not in his nature. Neither of us likes to be alone.

"And you'd be fine… if Seth is fine, him being on his own with the baby?"

"Yes. I just know Seth will need help, is all…"

I imagine Seth holding a little baby boy. He's always been so protective and he's nothing like the reckless youth he used to be. "He'll make a good dad. He wants to be a dad."

"So you just want me to be the cool aunt?" she jokes and the dark clouds around her slowly fade. "That was the plan anyway."

"I guess…" I can't help but smile just a hint of a grin. "Seth sometimes doesn't respond well. Like the last time I left. And I just want to make sure everything will be all right."

A sarcastic laugh leaves her in a huff as she lifts up the menu, her eyes wide with humor. "Is that what you call it?"

She has to keep talking before I fully grasp what she's getting at.

"Jase told me about what he did when you left him last time. Not that it was… not that it's the same."

"Right," I answer the single word, any bit of hunger vanishing as the conversation progresses.

"Marcus called him the black widower in the letters," she comments, her gaze on the menu.

"They're still going through them?" I question her. Truth be told, I'm curious to read them. I'm more anxious for Delilah to show up. Any day now. And I'm reluctant to quit for that one reason. Delilah has to know who Marcus is. Or at least what he looks like. I know Seth told me not to concern myself with it, but she could help them if only she told them—or me—who Marcus is or anything about how to find him.

"Yeah, there are a lot of them, years' worth, and a lot of decoding."

It's quiet as we both stare down at the menus. The ding of the front door opening, the din of chatter and clink of silverware on dishes is our backdrop.

"I'll put it in the paperwork," I tell her, taking in a deep breath and feeling more at peace. More ready for whatever may happen. "That you'll have secondary custody."

"Paperwork?"

"I want my affairs in order." Everything from a will to life insurance is updated. Absolutely every *I* dotted and *T* crossed. "We'll sign them on Thursday."

Dropping the menu, I stare back at Bethany, only to see that look back on her face, the solemn one.

"Thursday it is then."

I nod in agreement and say, "Thursday."

It's easy to talk about some things with Bethany and some things with Seth. Other things are best to keep to myself.

Tossing the keys onto the foyer table, I take in the crowded living room. Boxes and more cardboard boxes filled with things from my old apartment are taking up so much space, and here I am, adding more bags to the mess.

"Seth?" I call out and the plastic crinkles as I set the last bag down with the rest of them.

My feet ache and my back feels a bit like shit, to put it eloquently, but there's so much work to do.

"Babe?" I call out louder and peer down the hallway, which is lined by boxes too.

There's a single light on down the hall, coming from the room that we decided would be the nursery.

He always calls out when I'm home. It's odd. I know his mind is elsewhere with everything going on but still.

My steps are careful as I walk quietly down the hall. Thoughts of the blonde, of Marcus, of every bad thought that keeps me up at night make me second-guess going down the hall at all.

The faint thuds in my chest get harsher and I call out, my voice a bit shaky, "Seth."

The sight of him, poking his head out of the room, his brow furrowed and a headphone dangling from one ear while the other's still firmly in place eases the fear that was running through me.

"You all right?" he questions me, concern changing to protectiveness as he strides confidently down the hall, taking the earbuds out completely.

"Yeah, I just… I'm home." I stumble over my words, feeling foolish, but when I say I'm home and Seth's eyes light up, his hard features soften and he leans down, both hands finding their place on my lower back, his lips brushing against mine… well there's nothing foolish about that.

With my hands against his hard muscles, everything inside of me melts. A small hum escapes me when he breaks the short-lived kiss but then bends down to nip my neck. My head falls back and I could stay there just with him, in a crowded hallway full of boxes, forever.

"Let me show you what I've been doing." He's too eager to move me, even though my feet are planted firmly where they are in protest.

I let him lead me away, taking my hand. His is so strong, so large it wraps wholly around mine.

"It's paint that's safe for babies. That's what the clerk said. And for you," Seth informs me before the room comes fully into view.

"It's mostly dried," he says and lets go of my hand as I walk into the brightly lit bedroom that smells faintly of fresh paint. The former modern fan has been replaced with one that has alternating blue- and white-colored blades. A dark navy blue compared to the pale blue on the far wall, the one with the bay window.

I can't speak as I take it all in. The pile of cardboard in the one corner, the newly built whitewashed crib and matching dresser. I almost step on a screwdriver; Seth grabs my waist to pull me back. Pulling me into his embrace, warm and strong and everything I could ever want.

"I know it's a mess, but I'll clean it up tonight after I finish putting the rest together."

"It's so beautiful. I love it. You did all this?" I say and turn in his embrace, still stunned and so overwhelmed.

"Yeah, I needed something to do." His answer comes with a handsome smile, a charming one, but it doesn't reach his pale blue eyes.

"You all right?"

He starts to say yes, I can hear it without the word even being spoken, but shifting his gaze to an empty box that needs to be broken down, he leaves me where I am and gets to work, doing just that, breaking down the cardboard with a box cutter so it lays flat.

"I'm good with us. Good with this. Just," he pauses and takes in a deep breath, stretching out his shoulders with his back to me. The white shirt stretches tight over his shoulders and it's then that I see a bit of paint he got on it. Seth looks handsome in suits, but he was made to be blue collar. In those jeans, with those muscles. No suit, expensive fabric and tailored perfectly or not, is justified to hide all that.

"Just what?" I ask him and make myself busy too, grabbing the stack of white wicker baskets laying on the corner of the floor by other bags of baby items and lining them up on the dresser. There are a few empty plastic bags scattered around the room, so I pick them each up, balling them up and putting the smaller ones inside of the largest.

"I'm messed up right now," he admits, his voice lower than usual.

I pause what I'm doing, watching him as he keeps working, not looking back at me.

"Can I do anything?" I offer, silently praying, no—begging, God please let there be something I can do. I hate seeing him like this.

"No," he answers, sitting back on his heels, wiping his forehead with the back of his hand. I watch as he takes a moment to look at the crib, a genuine smile slipping onto his face, but it's gone in a moment. With his head hung low, he grabs another box and continues what he was doing.

"What's wrong?" I dare to ask, not bothering to do anything now. Instead I find a clear spot in the corner of the room, sitting on the floor and trying to get comfortable.

The second my ass hits the ground, Seth looks up. "I ordered that rocker that matches the crib. The one you wanted," he tells me and my heart does a little flip. "It's delayed but it'll be here next weekend."

I love him like this. For some reason, it gets me all choked up and my eyes glaze over a bit when I smile and whisper my thanks. "That can't be what's wrong, though? A rocking chair getting you like this?" I try to keep it light. My arms wrap around my knees and I curve my back, stretching out my sore muscles.

"Marcus told me to do something I don't want to do."

His answer both surprises me and sends alarm

shooting through me. That cautious feeling that came over me when I first came home, comes back with full force.

"What is it?"

"I can't tell you and I don't want you to stress. I just need you to know that I'm off right now, and I'm doing my best to be here for you how you need me. If I seem out of it, it's because of that, not because of us. I love us. I want to be here for you."

"Well why you?" The second question comes out even faster. Why is Marcus involved? Why is he telling Seth to do anything? I hate him in this moment. He doesn't scare me. That's what happens when anger takes over. Nothing scares you when you're angry.

"Delilah will come back to the center—" I can't finish because Seth cuts me off.

"Babygirl," he says and pauses, crawling over to where I am to put his hands on my shoulders, staring into my eyes. "I promise you, I'll figure it out. I just don't like what I have to do."

My inhale is unsteady until he leans down and kisses my cheek. My eyes close and when they do, he kisses me tenderly, surprising me when his lips mold to mine.

He breaks the kiss, and my eyes stay closed as he whispers into the warm air between us, "That's what I needed. That's all I need."

The cool air surrounds me the moment he leaves me, going back to piling the last of the cardboard before grabbing a box that holds some other sort of crib that we're supposed to have. One that's portable and rocks.

"I have more too," I tell him and force myself to get up and get the bags so I can organize all the little things in drawers and baskets.

Seth is quiet as I leave, but he looks over his shoulder to give me a look that warms me from head to toe. It's the kind of look where you know the other person wants you, that they love you, and that if they could, they'd lay with you forever.

My fingers brush against my lips when I get to the hall; I can still feel his kiss there. And I know I'm blushing because my cheeks are warm.

We work in silence for a little while, me taking things out of the bags and plopping them into the newly designated baskets for such items. Binkies, rattles, bath toys. I did end up buying nearly half of the ones on that display.

"Oh." The sight of the bath toys makes my eyes go wide when I remember.

"What? Are you okay?" Seth answers quick and I'd laugh at the look on his face if it wasn't so heartwarming.

"He kicked today," I answer him and all those emotions come back.

His gaze moves to my lower belly. "If he does it again, I'll tell you," I offer and a handsome grin stretches across his face.

He crawls over to me, such an odd thing for a powerful man like him to do. Lowering his lips to my belly and slipping his hands up my shirt, he whispers for little prince to wake up and give him a kick.

He jokes that it's not fair that "Mom" got to feel it without him. He called me Mom.

I wish he was the biological father. I wish there was no backup plan needed and I knew for certain everything was going to be just fine.

But even if those wishes don't come true, I still feel so damn lucky. At that thought, Seth pulls back, his hands still on my belly, just a split second after a small kick lands near my ribs.

Seth's stubbled jaw drops in awe. "He did it. That was him?" he asks me.

Nodding my head, I whisper, yeah, and watch him watch my belly, telling our son to do it again.

He doesn't, but that only prods Seth to kiss my belly. Right where the kick was.

"Thought he might take the chance to get me." He mumbles the joke and it makes me laugh.

"Thank you for doing this."

"Of course."

I can't stop myself from asking as he rubs soothing circles on my bump, "Why can't we smile like this all the time? Just have this forever?" It was meant to be rhetorical, but Seth answers me.

"Because I am terrified to lose you. And I have a lot of reasons to believe I might."

"If it's up to me, you won't. You know I'm a fighter." I barely whisper my promise.

He only smiles at me before kissing my belly and then the tip of my nose.

"I love you."

He responds with a hand splayed across my lower stomach, "I love us."

"God is so unfair," I groan.

"Why?"

"Because you're fucking perfect."

He's on me in an instant. His lips hot against mine, his hands traveling down the curve of my waist and then lower.

"Seth," I say and his name is a gasp on my lips, stolen between a heated kiss. Emotions swirl with an ever-present desire and all my sadness drowns in it.

Every nerve ending between my legs sparks with recognition and need.

My breath is his, his mouth never leaving mine, even as his forearm braces my back. Lowering me to the ground.

Desperation would have me ripping his clothes off, needing to be one with him in this very instant. Every second is torturous as Seth does just the opposite.

His fingers barely graze my skin as he undresses me slowly, one piece at a time. And he does the same for himself, not letting me move an inch beneath him. With his body above mine, I'm never cold, always warmed and protected.

If his lips ever leave mine, they travel down my jaw, my neck, my collarbone, leaving a tender trail that's ravenous just the same.

"I need you," I whimper and Seth pulls back, staring down at me with complete devotion. There's a sadness that swirls deep in the depths of his gaze, but it's gone as quickly as it came. His voice is filled with wretched emotion when he says, "I wish I could go back and tell you every day that I loved you. Every day."

"Seth," I say, trying to comfort him, but when my hands cup his strong jaw, he takes them by the wrist. He kisses my palms and then plants them above my head. Lowering his lips to mine, he whispers, "Know that if I have one regret in this life, it's that I didn't tell you I loved you every single day I could have."

My fingers spear in his hair, but before I can give him a response, he devours me as only Seth can.

He enters me in one swift motion. My neck arches as the sweet pain of being stretched stirs with the hungered need for more.

I wish I could meet his pace, but he alternates between deep, slow thrusts and a pistoning every time I come close to the edge. He doesn't hold back like I expect him to when I get there. He forces me over, screaming out his name as my orgasm tears through me. And then he slows, pushing himself deeper until he's pressed against my back wall, groaning his need for release in the crook of my neck.

Over and over he takes me, until my throat is sore from crying out his name and my body trembles with overwhelming pleasure.

CHAPTER 12

Seth

"I WANT TO ASK YOU SOMETHING," I SAY AND MY VOICE comes out stronger than I'd like, breaking up the peaceful silence. Her eyes open and she peers up at me through her thick lashes. I knew she wasn't sleeping. Neither of us have been able to sleep, and for good reason. We have these moments that are pure happiness, but then reality dampens them.

She rolls on her side, the bed groaning as she does and the dim light kissing along her bare skin emphasizes every curve as she turns to give me her full attention.

"Yes?" Her barely spoken question fills up the master bedroom.

I've never been anxious to ask her anything. Never in my life. But the truth she has for me could cut me deeper than any knife would.

"You've been asking me lots of things. A lot of hard questions." I'm fully aware that I'm stalling. I fucking hate what this situation has done to me.

"I know. I promise I've asked all of them. No more hard questions." She promises me as if she's done something wrong by asking them.

Licking my lower lip, I settle my hand on her lower back over the thin sheet and kiss the tip of her nose.

With my forehead resting against hers I whisper, "You can ask me anything you want, whenever you want. Hard or not."

She nods ever so slightly and then lifts up her lips, kissing the tip of my nose just as I've done to her.

"What is it?" she asks.

"The father… do you know who he is?" Although we're both so still, and the room itself is eerily quiet, my pulse races and my blood rushes in my ears.

"I have an idea. I just haven't reached out." She reaches for the sheet, bringing it up higher like I knew she would. Putting anything she can between herself and that question. "I don't plan on it until after the baby's here."

"Do you have to?" I ask her and there's not an ounce of anger or authority there. It's a simple question, one that aches inside my chest. I don't let her hear it in my voice, or see it on my expression, but I know she knows. She always knows.

"I haven't decided," she whispers quietly. The vulnerability that I keep hidden away, she wears openly. I know if she does, she'll never hear back. But still, I don't want him to be on her mind. I just want it to be us. Only us for her.

Readjusting on the bed, I pull her closer to me and kiss her gently. Keeping my eyes closed, I ask her, "Did you enjoy it? What you had with him? Or any of the men you were with while we weren't together?"

The second the question is spoken, I know I've officially gone mad. I'm fucked up and nowhere near the man I once was.

But if that's what she had while I wasn't there, I want to know she was happy. I need to know that much.

"That feels like a loaded question," she says. This time she's the one stalling, staring back at me as if she's not sure if she should tell me the truth.

"He didn't hurt you, right?" I ask, rolling onto my back, pulling away and pinching the bridge of my nose. I'm so fucking weak and helpless. I've never hated myself more.

The sheets rustle as she props herself up, placing a palm against my chest. She stares down at me.

"No. No, none of them hurt me in any way. It was… it was just a hookup mostly. I don't know what you want me to say." Her last statement is spoken nervously.

"Did they break your heart?" I ask her, finally pulling my hand away to look back at her.

"They never had it to break." She'll never know what her answer does to me. How much it means but how much it hurts just the same.

I give her a weak smile that I'm not sure she can see in the darkness. "I guess I'll let them live then."

She utters the smallest of laughs and says, "Is that why you asked?"

"I don't know," I answer her honestly. "I don't know a lot anymore when I used to know everything."

"My broken king," Laura whispers, kissing the dip in my throat.

"My broken queen," I say in reply, not knowing how true a title that is for her until the words have escaped into the air.

A beep from my phone interrupts the moment. Leaving my scattered thoughts where they are, I kiss her knuckles before removing her hand from where it lays on my chest and reaching over to my phone.

"I have to go, Babygirl." It's the notification for the meeting tonight. For what must be done. I plant a kiss on her lips before reminding both myself and her, "Security's outside."

"I know," she answers with a small smile that doesn't reach her eyes. The blues of them carry so much depth of emotion as she stares back at me.

"I'll be back as soon as I can."

"I know."

I cup her face, feeling her warmth and running my thumb over her kissable lips. "I love you," I tell her.

"I know. And I love you too."

I know she does. That's why I have to do this. Whatever it takes, I'll do it for her.

It's almost three a.m. and the bar is just winding down. The music's off since it's closing time and the only patrons left are ones who have business outside of liquor consumption.

Anthony is behind the bar. He's the first one I see, drying glasses with a bright white dishrag as I walk through the front door. The man I want to see has his back to me, seated on a stool just to the right of Anthony. Just like last time. I don't want this setup to become anything more than what it is. A one-time exchange of information.

With a nod, I give the order for him to move to the other side of the bar. Five men are in the main room right now, with maybe two more in the back. All of them are men who work in this bar, and therefore for the Cross brothers, and then there's Officer Walsh and myself.

"I was just getting ready to order another," Walsh comments as I approach. No doubt the sound of my footsteps alerted him. "Do you need a drink too?" he questions, his voice dull. Which is appropriate for the occasion.

He knows exactly what I'm doing. Giving Marcus a firm yes or no. Setting everything into motion, as he likes to say.

The legs of the stool scrape on the ground as I pull it out, taking the one to the left of Walsh. He doesn't move his pale blue gaze from the back of the bar. The reflection in them shows the rows of colored glasses in front of us.

"I'll have one with you. Just one, though."

He nods, swallowing thickly and then motions toward Anthony. His gaze darts between Walsh and me until I nod. He's a damn good kid, learning quick, but I feel for him. One day, he'll be in the same place I am. It always comes down to this. Making deals to save the ones you love.

"What are we having?" I ask Walsh even though I see

Anthony pull out an amber bottle of what I know is expensive whiskey.

Walsh waves me off and says, "Doesn't matter. I'm buying."

The two shots thud on the bar as Anthony sets them down in front of us. Walsh lifts his in salute and I toast mine against his before throwing back the neat whiskey.

"He wasn't always like this; you know?" Walsh starts, his gaze still focused in front of us. He hasn't even looked at me yet.

I square my shoulders toward him and that does the trick. His eyes are red, with dark bags underneath. With his dark jeans, a t-shirt with some sort of logo on it, and a black leather jacket, he has the look of a man on the edge. On the edge of losing it all.

"There was a time when we saw eye to eye. When it was only the criminals and men who killed for sport who were on his radar. And then… one case… one case changed everything."

He holds up two fingers, indicating two shots and I tell him just one. His response is that both are for him.

"It was then that he decided even the smallest of crimes could lead to something horrific that needed to be prevented."

"What was the case?"

He looks like he's going to answer me, but instead he puts a shot to his lips, throwing it back and fiddling with the glass.

"It was five years ago. In all fairness, it changed me

too." His gaze turns distant and he tosses back the second shot.

I nearly ask him what Marcus wanted from him at the warehouse. But he slams the shot glass down and then faces me to ask, "Do you have it?"

I can only nod, the temperature of my blood getting hotter and hotter as he holds his hand out, waiting. If I do this, I know there's no going back. If I don't, I don't know that Laura will live and she has to live. She has to make it through this.

"Yeah," I finally answer him, desperation making me sick to my stomach.

Walsh's gaze falls slightly, looking something like disappointment when I grab the envelope from my back pocket, folded and creased in half, and hand it to him, although I don't let go of it.

"Are you sure you want to do this?" he questions in a breath just above a whisper, still not looking at me.

"Like he said," I say as I remember what Marcus told us in that warehouse, "I'm aware of everything I have to lose, and I won't risk her." I may hate myself, but if I don't, I know with everything in me that I'll lose her. By the hand of the devil named Marcus, or by the hand of God.

So this has to happen.

"You made your choice then?" he asks and attempts to take the thin envelope, so thin it nearly looks empty, but I still can't let go of it.

"Yeah," I answer him and finally let go, releasing it and taking the consequences in return.

"Then this is for you," Walsh says simply, reaching inside of his jacket. I watch the men reach for their guns, but Walsh doesn't pay attention. He retrieves an envelope, just as thin. "For what it's worth, I believe him. If he says he can save her, he can and he will."

I nod at his statement. "I do too," I confess, my voice turning tight. "It's the only reason I agreed to this."

CHAPTER 13

Laura

I'VE NEVER GIVEN NOTICE OF LEAVE BEFORE. I'VE never quit. I hadn't realized that until just now as I get in my car to go to the Rockford Center and do just that.

It's all I can think about on the drive there. How much I busted my ass for this job. How it's my first real job. How much I love it and what I do and my patients.

The roads are icy and even though I'm fully aware of that, I nearly fall on my ass when I open the car door to go in and tell Aiden I have to quit. *Shit.* My grip on the edge of the door is so tight, I'm able to hoist myself up and grateful the door itself didn't snap off.

Thump, thump, thump, my heart races along with the wind whipping at my face and destroying the limited effort I put into making my hair look semi-decent.

Just breathe.

In and out, I focus on breathing. The morning air is nippy, but it feels worse than that. Everything just feels wrong. Everything feels off.

"I'm not quitting," I whisper into the frosty air, the words turning into fog in front of my face.

"This isn't running and this isn't giving up." I finally find my footing and stand up straighter, more relaxed and calm. More sure of myself as I stare at the building I've practically lived in for years now.

It's only a temporary leave, I promise myself.

The damn wind isn't quite as bad when I finally close the door. The resounding bang of it closing seems too final. It all feels too final as I stand there, so I slip my hands into my pockets and wait. Just for a moment. Nothing in this life is final. I know that, but why does it feel like it is?

Cars drive by the busy road to the right of the center. A few here and a few there, but the parking lot at the Rockford Center is mostly empty.

It's a Wednesday morning, so no deliveries are scheduled. And with the holidays coming, everyone seems to have already taken a bit of vacation themselves.

It's slower, colder, and the bitterness of it all is getting to me. Winter isn't my season. I may have been born in winter, but it doesn't like me much. And I don't like it either.

It's as if everything is smothered, everything depressed in some way during this season. I'm not a fan and neither is my shaky mentality.

Even with my hands in my pockets of my black wool coat, the heaviest coat I have, they're freezing. So I force myself to move, one step and then another. Tomorrow I'll find my gloves, wherever I've put them.

The thud in my chest doesn't quit. My boots click on the sidewalk and my heart beats with it. That is until I hear my name, called from my right.

The chill bites down all the way to the bone as I stand there, staring at her vision through the clouded fog of my breath.

"Delilah." I call out her name but it's ragged and cut short. I have to clear my throat and this time I walk faster, to the edge of the roundabout at the front of the building where she's standing.

A mix of emotions overwhelm me but the first is relief that she's checking in. I will always love my patients. Then quickly the reality comes back, falling like a building that's collapsed. One floor buckles, then it's slow for a moment, disbelief kicks in, then the whole damn thing crashes down.

Delilah, Marcus, the threats, the letters. I don't know what to do but she can't leave. I can't let her leave.

"Delilah," I call out her name louder, her on one side of the street while I'm on the other.

"Miss Roth," she calls to me and her voice is confident and comes with a recollection of nostalgia. As if we're old friends.

Her thick red coat falls to her calves, hiding the tops of her leather boots. She always looks like New York. Not just like any New Yorker, but this woman gives off an energy that represents NYC itself. I told her that the first time I met her. That she looked like New York. Even though that night she wasn't nearly as put together as she is now.

"I was hoping to see you," she tells me as she gets closer, checking both her right and left side as she crosses the street. One would think she's a powerful woman, capable and confident. But depression doesn't know a social status and I can't tell just from a simple conversation how she's faring either.

"I'm so glad you're here." The words rush out of me as the wind whips by again, blowing strands of my hair into my face. Hers stays where she put it, high in a perfectly arranged bun on the top of her head. All I can think is that she's seen Marcus. If I could convince her to tell me his full name, or to talk to a sketch artist if she doesn't know it… if only I could do that, I'm sure it could help. I've never been surer of anything.

Her red lips complement her dark skin and her auburn eyes stare back with the hint of the smile she wears on her feminine face.

"Are you leaving?" I ask her, finding the cold wrap itself around me tighter and tighter as the tip of my nose seems to freeze.

"I was just making an appointment. I didn't check myself in this time but I thought it'd be wise to come in for a consultation."

I nod subconsciously, knowing she needs to do that for her prescription as well.

"I—I agree," I say, forgetting my predicament for a moment. But then I think twice. My place is beside Seth. My place is with him and what he needs. I owe it to him to at least try. "I need your help with something."

"Can I ask if it's for professional or personal reasons?" Her question catches me off guard, but only for a moment.

"So you know that personally—"

"That our respective personal worlds are no longer…" she trails off as her smile falters and a flash of a woman I used to know, a woman I used to hold as she cried, flickers in the swirls of amber.

"A dear friend told me how you're involved now. You know what I know. I don't have to say it. And I respect him and his wishes. He's only ever tried to help me. You know that, don't you? I'm sorry, but I can't help you if it's about that."

"Please, I just need you to tell me who Marcus is or what he looks like. Please, he's—"

The smile she gives me doesn't reach her glossy eyes when she says, "I've been told not to speak to you any longer." Her voice is choked when she cuts me off. "But I am so happy to see you." She pulls a tissue from her pocket, dabbing at the corner of her eyes and looking to her left and right rather than at me, before telling me she should go.

I'm speechless. I've stayed up with her for hours on countless nights by her side while she needed me. I only need this one thing. Just this one and then the man I love won't keep himself busy, his mind focused on a task this

Marcus wants him to do. "Wait," I call out and grab her wrist, the pain and agony mixing like a potent cocktail with the anguish.

"Marcus. Just tell me who he is. Please, please?" I'm not above begging. "He's hurting my family." It's the truth and she must know it is.

She doesn't show any reaction, she doesn't acknowledge what I've said, but she does look down slowly at where I'm holding her. As if to warn me that I better let go.

"You know me as a person who wants to see you whole and healthy. Someone who's kept your secrets." I let go of her, but her gaze is steady as I continue, the wind turning icy. "But there's a side of me that comes out when it has to. A side that I hate and a side that I don't want to come out. I need your help and if I'd had it, so much would have been prevented."

"Oh, dear girl, none of it would have been prevented. Not a damn bit of it."

"I killed someone." I whisper the confession, and I know it's not lost in the wind because of the sadness that echoes in her eyes. No shock, no fear, only sadness.

"I can't help you." That's all she gives me.

"I can't let you leave. I need your help," I say and desperation flutters in my tone.

"You don't need me…" she says, lowering her voice before she continues knowingly, "a man does."

"A man I love," I correct her, raising my voice, and then feel foolish and like a petulant child.

My hand covers my mouth and the fear that I'm going

to fail comes over me. She's really not going to help me. She's not going to help us.

Before I can explain anything to her, before I can beg her to let me take her out for coffee and could we just talk, she stares into my eyes with a piercing gaze that only comes from a woman who's been to hell and back.

"Yes, a man you love, a man you'd do anything for and he'd do the same for you… Even things you both know are so very wrong. I know that story. I know it well." Her eyes are riddled with a mix of emotions as she whispers, "Do you want me to tell you how it ends?"

Her bottom lip trembles and mine does the same as I stare at her, so clearly in agony.

"Please," I beg her once more.

"He told me not to speak to you," she says softly, with remorse.

Shaking my head, I turn from her, my head spinning and not knowing what to do. What's right and wrong. But knowing I have to tell Seth she's here, I hurt for her the most. It all runs through my mind, every scenario, every fear… until I hear the squeal of tires.

"Laura!" Delilah's voice is heard so clearly. Everything slows. I don't realize it's a car at first. It's just a blur of red. I didn't even realize I was in the street.

The roads are icy.

The brakes aren't working.

Thud. Thud.

My heart stops working… the third thud never coming as the car crashes into me and I tumble over it. My thigh hits first, my body's limp, maybe from shock, I'm not sure. It's all so cold, so sharply violent.

I know that I tumble over the hood and land on the asphalt, unforgivingly hard. The pain is immediate, but it doesn't feel real. None of it feels real until I see Delilah standing over me, but looking at something else, someone else, screaming to call an ambulance.

CHAPTER 14

Seth

I USED TO REVEL IN THESE MOMENTS. THE TALK OF THE business, the exchange of money. I wanted to know all the ins and outs of every deal. I craved the power of it all.

But as I sit in this room, Carter's office in the Cross brothers' estate, I can't stand to be here.

My thumb keeps tapping on the hardwood armrest of the walnut chair. My mind keeps racing. I imagine this is what men look like when they have something to hide. Exactly what I look like now. And ever since that warehouse meeting, it's been getting worse and worse. Every day, I break down more as I come to terms with it. If only I could tell them, but Marcus needs to go through with his promise. I won't say shit to anyone until she's healthy and safe.

I'll do it for her. I'd do anything for her.

"And what about Nikolai? We just let him leave?"

Jase questions Carter about men in the upper west area of our territory. Each section is essentially cut into fourths and the income that comes and goes is analyzed, problems sorted, men, police and drugs alike. I can't focus on a damn thing.

There isn't one topic I've spoken up about. Not even the bar.

"What happened at the warehouse?" Carter's deep voice breaks through my racing thoughts. It's at that moment when my phone rings. I silence it without looking, unable to look away from Carter's dark gaze as he broods in his chair behind the large desk. Placing it on vibrate, I answer him, "Nothing that concerns you. It was about Laura."

The sky is white and angry behind him in the large paned windows. It only makes him look that much more foreboding. I don't fear him; there isn't anything I fear right now more than losing Laura.

I feel remorse for all of them. But they'll understand. When it's done and over with, they'll understand. I trust that they'll follow through accordingly.

"Bullshit," he bites out.

"We know something happened." Jase's voice is calmer, less threatening as he leans back in the seat across from me, both of us on the other side of Carter's desk. Declan's across the room. He likes to sit there, in the back corner near the books.

"Walsh is leaving. He retired. So Marcus told him

something," Jase prods, and I can feel all three of them staring at me. Wanting answers.

I don't look at the roaring fireplace with intricately carved marble; I don't glance down at the expensive rug beneath my feet. My gaze moves easily from Carter to Jase as I tell them I'm not privy to what was said when I left.

"All I know is that Marcus wants a meet and that he traded information about Laura's health for me to make it happen."

It's not all a lie, but it's not all the truth either.

"Right," Jase says then drops his head and his gaze. "I know I've said it before," he says as his foot taps on the rug, creating a dull thump each time that mirrors the sound in my chest. "But if there's anything we can do..."

"There's nothing," I answer them and carefully breathe in and out. Marcus said he could.

He said he'd come through first. And then, I come through for him.

I'll save her first. Gentleman's honor. That's his promise. Once she's saved, the events are put in motion. Then I'll tell them. One way or another.

The letter is already written.

My phone rings again, vibrating in my hand.

I clear my throat, wanting to give them something. I feel like a rat, sitting here with them, with men I respect, men who have been there for me and I've been there for them.

"I get the idea that you're hiding something," Carter prods and a sick smile kicks up my lips when I look back at him.

The air between us all is different now. It feels thicker, heated, suffocating.

"I am," I admit to him, but I don't elaborate.

"If Marcus made you a deal—" Jase starts to say but then his phone vibrates loud on the desk and he has to silence it.

"I want to tell you, but I can't… it doesn't concern you anyway." I add the last part more for reassurance than anything. Even though it's not true.

I know what happens to men who keep secrets. Men who admit them are signing a death wish. I won't lie more than I have to, but I can't tell them.

"You're really going to keep something from me?" Carter questions and for a moment, a small moment in the silence of this room, surrounded by three men who would kill me, three men who are positioned all the way around me, all carrying guns, I fear they will.

It's gone quickly and it's the first time I've felt it, not because it's the first time Carter has thrown his weight around, but because for the first time, I can't die. I have to follow through on my deal with Marcus. If I die, there's no way in hell he'll save her.

"I ask that you trust me. That's all I ask. I'll tell you everything when I can."

"Tell us what?" Declan questions, then his phone goes off and so does mine again. They're both only on vibrate, but all of us notice in the tense room.

Irritation mars Carter's face, creating hard lines in his features. "It's about Marcus and Walsh and I'll be damned if that doesn't involve us."

Jase and him share a look before he says, "You can tell us anything."

"I will. When it's time."

Carter's fist slams down but as it does, his own phone rings, the shrill sound of the tone filling up the room.

"What the fuck is it?" Carter roars, clearly pissed from my insolence. I'm only doing what must be done and I know damn well he'd do it too.

His expression falls as silence overcomes him. When his gaze lands on me, I know it's bad. Not in the way he elicits fear, but in the way that's often followed with "I'm so sorry about your loss." I know it's Laura. I know it is from the look on his face.

"Take this." Carter's tone is full of remorse and a sick gut-wrenching feeling comes over me. I don't know how I even stand and take the call.

"Hello," I answer and swallow thickly, prepared for whatever happens, silently praying I'm wrong. That she's just fine. But I wasn't prepared for the sound of Bethany's choked voice or her sobs.

"It's Laura."

CHAPTER 15

Laura

I T's ALL IN AND OUT. A WHITE HAZE FLOODS MY VISION and my eyes are so heavy. There's a pounding in my head but it flows through every inch of me and it hurts. Well, for a moment, and then…

I know it hurts, but more than anything I'm tired and my body feels light, not in pain. There is no agonizing feeling. All it is, is falling.

The stark white walls of the hospital fade and so does the chaos of yelling and the man barking out orders above me, his white coat open, his baby blue scrubs taking up all the space as he leans over me… it all blurs and I don't mind. His stubble comes into focus and then out, his hazel eyes seem to hover over me and then it's all gone and I fade into them.

Because I'm falling and it's so light, it's so easy. It's comforting to let everything fade and blur and then there's silence in a rush of peace.

But then I'm back again. Bright white lights, screaming and the pain.

In and out.

"Keep up compressions," one voice says, or rather demands.

"It's thready but it's there." A woman's comment is rushed, panicked.

I suck in a breath, my eyes going wide. *No, make it stop!* Fuck, the pain is all-consuming. I can't move, even as I feel like I'm choking and the instinct to grab my throat takes over, I can't move. Something holds me down and it digs into my skin.

Help me, it hurts so fucking much.

"Miss Roth, Miss Roth." Someone's calling for me, talking over the storm of worry that thunders with every sound in the elevator. "We're taking you up to surgery."

"What happened?" I swear I speak the question aloud but he talks over me. My throat hurts. Why does my throat hurt? What happened? Why does everything hurt? A deep crease runs down my forehead and I try to move, to turn over, but I can't.

"You're in good hands," he says and his statement comes with a ding of the elevator. "Let's move!" his voice booms.

In an effort to get a grip on reality, I lift my head only to be met with the dizzying need to lie back down. Be still. In this moment, I want to fall again. I don't want this.

A striking pulse of pain, as if in anger at my thoughts, races from my heart up my chest. A strangled cry leaves me as I writhe in agony.

The car. The accident. It floods back in a hurried tumble.

"My baby," I whimper, my expression crumpled. It's only a whisper forced into a plea for something. To stop this. *Make it stop*, I pray as my throat tightens and tears leak from the corners of my eyes. *Please, I only want to fall.*

The hot tear rolls down my cheek and the salt meets my lips as I cry out again in pain. I can't move and that makes it worse. Everything hurts. Every moment, every thought. Every breath steals strength from me.

Make it stop. Please, please.

My memory whirls with thoughts of how I got here, but with the pounding I can't remember it all. I don't know what happened. It's in and out and I can't hold on to it.

Where's Seth? I want to cry out for him. He's still with me, isn't he? Seth would never leave me. Seth is here. He has to be. I cry out his name, Seth, but he doesn't answer.

"We're losing her," a voice says. She sounds young and scared. My head falls to the left as I sob through another bolt of aching pain.

It's my heart. My heart. *Did I go to the doctor's?* I can't remember. *Did I tell him about my heart?* The way it pitter-patters.

Slowly I remember the doctor. And then leaving.

Leaving the woman who was dressed for a date, so distracted. I remember her. I remember coming home. *Cami. Cami.* "No, no," I scream a hollow sound that I don't recognize, tearing at the restraints holding me down.

"You have to stay calm, Miss Roth, calm down!" they yell. Both at me and at each other.

Cami. Other memories rush back to me.

It takes me a moment, watching the fluorescent lights blur above me as we're rushed down the hall. One deep breath. The white and silver blend into a pattern as a prick hits my arm. I barely notice it. Another deep breath. It's the chill of whatever they've shot me with that brings the action to my attention.

My eyes burn, but my body relaxes. On the third breath I can't even feel the rise of my chest anymore.

My blood chills and with a deep inhale, I remember. That was years ago. It's been years.

Fuck, why does that make it hurt even deeper? A heaviness weighs down on me, and with it, a numbness in my toes and fingers.

I ran. The memory forces the tears to flow easier, harder, although I'm silent. Watching the years of my life come and go in waves.

I left him.

No. No! He's here. I know he's here. "Seth!" I scream out, knowing I can't live without him. I could never be without him. My head shakes and strong hands object to the movement. There are yells and demands but I don't hear any of them because they aren't Seth's voice. He's not here. Seth, I murmur pathetically. Pathetic, painful, lonely. My voice echoes all the mournful emotions. I don't want to be alone. I could never bear it if the last person I ever said I love you to wasn't Seth King.

Memories flash. His hands on my wrists, his lips on my neck. Seth, I whisper to no one. He's not for them.

I remember now, the last weeks coming slower, more detailed. I can feel him, his hard body and the heat of his embrace.

Seth. I don't bother saying his name. It's not for them. It's for me.

The car is the last thing I see. Delilah and the shock, the fear that rolled through me and with the impact, my body jolts and another wave of pain.

My head is heavy, and so are my eyes. It's cold, freezing cold as goosebumps dance along my skin. The loud ringing in my ears is unbearable and then suddenly the noise is faint, soothing. It's not so cold anymore.

It's only as cold as the breeze when I fall.

I recognize her voice. The doctor. My doctor. Doctor Tabor.

Fuck, the pain. With the recognition of a voice, the pain comes back. I feel it first, then the ringing. It's so loud. The pounding, the ringing, the screaming pain.

Blinking rapidly, the lights come back. Everything whirls and falls back into place. No, no, let it be over.

"Miss Roth," she says and the force in her voice grips

me. I know her voice. Her hair is pulled back tight, making her look even thinner, even frailer, although I know her to be an imposing force with the strong will she has.

The light in my eye is blinding and I fall again.

"Laura, can you look at me?"

I know her voice. The doctor. My doctor.

I nod my head ever so slightly without moving my neck. I can't now, I can't move it. The brace is tight, but not constricting. I can breathe better. I can breathe.

It takes me a moment.

"Miss Roth, do you know where you are?"

Hospital. I don't know that I've spoken the answer until Dr. Tabor tells me that's correct.

"Do you know what happened?"

With the inhale, I wince from the pain and in an instant I'm moved from the gurney to a table, bright lights shining down in my eyes.

The headlights. The impact.

I can't breathe.

Car, the screech of tires. Delilah.

"Miss Roth, you were in a car accident and your injuries are severe."

Baby. My little prince.

I try to move my hands to my belly. He's not kicking. *Please kick.* Fear cripples me and they tell me to stop, but I can't see. Did the car hit my belly?

"My baby," I say and barely get the words out as my doctor hovers over my face. All I can see is her and her stern look although her eyes hold compassion.

"We're doing everything we can," she tells me, but her expression slips.

It lacks confidence because it lacks hope.

"Save my baby," I beg her but she doesn't listen. Someone else is talking. "My baby!" They don't listen.

"She needs a transplant right now." She answers someone else. She doesn't listen to me.

"Stay on the line with medical."

"They don't—"

"Keep calling," my doctor screams in response.

"We're going to do everything we can, Laura."

"My baby," I cry and I wish Seth were here. He'd fight for what I want. He'd tell them to save our son. He'd hold my hand. He would have hope.

"I'm going to do everything I can."

Did I tell him that I loved him? I can't remember. Did I at least tell him I loved him before I left?

CHAPTER 16

Seth

I'M SUPPOSED TO SIT HERE.

Tapping my phone against my suit pants in rapid succession, I stare down at the movement thinking, *How am I supposed to just sit here and do nothing?*

Gritting my teeth, I lean back in the simple chair and then stand up without conscious thought. I can't sit still.

I can't leave though.

There are fourteen wooden chairs in this room, all with squared backs and fabric with a navy pattern. It's like small petals scattered on them, I don't know. I've been staring at them for hours and I can't even say what they are.

Two rows of seven chairs, two long coffee tables between them and a large single-pane window on the far right. It's dark now that the sun's gone down. So it's just two black rectangular squares that I can see and the only light is from the fluorescent tubes above my head.

It's not supposed to happen like this.

Marcus promised he'd save her.

He swore he would.

Yet here I am, on death row with the Cross brothers, while Laura lies open on an operating table. And I can do nothing. This is my penance and I'll take it all and more, as long as they get to live.

When my hand starts trembling again, I shove the phone back into my pocket and pace.

My head is light from not breathing right. I can't do anything right. All I can hear is Bethany's voice when she called.

There was an accident.

Her cadence was full of dread and it ricochets in my mind, hitting every vulnerable place and with every impact, I see Laura, smiling, laughing, biting down on her lip as she peers up at me.

I just want her back like that. *Please, God.*

I've made a deal with the devil. I'll make one with God too.

I'll make every deal I can with every man in power on the face of this fucking earth if it means she gets to live.

"Hey, you want one?" Bethany asks, her voice small and quiet in the large room even though it's just the two of us.

"No thanks," I answer her as evenly as I can, even though dread seeps in regardless.

Her eyes are red and the mascara's no longer there where it was hours ago. She's barely moved from her seat. I don't know how she does it; I can't sit still at all. A few people have come into the room and saw her in scrubs so they approached her. Other than that, she's only gotten up to get coffee from a machine down the hall that takes two dollars to spew out an inferior form of caffeine.

"What about something else?" she asks me and when I look up at her splotchy face, I can see she's begging me to give her something to do, something to make it better. I can't tell her how much I relate. If only it was as easy as putting two wrinkled dollars into a machine.

"I could use a water maybe," I get out and the back of my eyes sting. I imagine they're red like hers.

"You might need some caffeine," she offers, a little more hopeful although the horrid look on her face doesn't change.

"I won't be able to sleep without knowing." Somehow I answer her without suffocating on that truth. On the possibility that it was all for nothing.

If she dies, I have no reason to live anyway.

"They should be able to tell us something. They should be here any minute to tell us she's all right." Jase's voice is unexpected. I didn't even hear him come up behind me. He's still in his stone-gray suit, jacket and everything. Mine's rumpled in comparison.

When Bethany falls into his arms, his kisses the top of her head before resting his chin on her crown and then looking at me.

"She's going to be all right. That's the only thing they'll say; that she made it. I know it, they have to," Bethany speaks into Jase's chest and I hear it.

"You okay?" Jase asks me and I only shake my head. I can't speak.

I want to thank him for just showing up. For being here for me in this dark time, but I don't deserve it. He knows it and so do I. After today? Things are going to be different between me and the Cross brothers. I know they are. And it was for nothing.

"She and our baby boy are going to be okay. They'll be all right." Bethany speaks as she wipes her eyes, breaking from her embrace with Jase. It's the first time she's broken down out here, although a few times, she's gone to the restroom and come out with her face much redder than before. "Your little prince, right?"

"Our little prince," I barely breathe, my hands trembling again.

"Still no word? Nothing?" Jase questions, and I can feel him looking at me but Bethany answers no, her hair swishing as she shakes her head.

She asks Jase if he wants a drink from the vending machine before leaving us alone.

"I just talked to Carter, he's coming with the guys." A chill flows over my shoulders.

I nod and think a moment before saying, "You know I would never do anything to risk you or any of you."

"I don't know what deal you made, but if he tried to kill her—"

I cut him off, realizing that he doesn't know. "It was Aiden's mother, the manager's mother." The words rush out but my inhale is slower, attempting to steady myself.

"Just an accident?" he questions with disbelief.

"The ice…" I can't finish. I saw the older woman, banged up and looking scared while she sobbed uncontrollably. "She was bringing him something for lunch."

Fuck, the pain. I hate it. I hate this.

But it's what I deserve, isn't it? They don't deserve it though. They don't deserve any of it.

"I've never been able to protect her." I speak without looking at Jase even though he sits down next to me. With my shoulders hunched over, I explain. "That's why I did it, why I planned it the way I did. Because I knew I couldn't protect her. I couldn't save her."

I see him lower himself, hunching like me, trying to look at me, but I don't let him. A hand covers my face.

"I would do anything for her, but I can't protect her."

"Say it." Jase's voice is firm.

"Say what?" I ask him, ready to say whatever he needs to hear. I don't have it in me to fight anymore. Whatever he wants to know, I'll tell him.

"Say she's going to be okay. Say she'll be fine." His words come out harsh but I can hear him swallow the pain down. "She's going to be okay and you need to say it."

I nod, even though I don't know that I believe it.

"She's going to make it," he says and he's firm.

"She has to." My eyes burn. "Both of them are going to be fine."

CHAPTER 17

Seth

IT WAS AN EIGHTEEN-HOUR SURGERY IN ALL. I SAT there, in that worn-out chair, staring at the pile of dog-eared magazines with torn pages and counting every second.

Jase is silent, apart from comforting Bethany.

There's a heavy weight on my chest that still won't let up. Even when the doctors came out, all three of them, the weight only got heavier.

They did all they could.

Beep, beep, beep.

The room is simple; there should be flowers in here. She loves flowers.

"Seth, is there anything…" Jase starts to ask as Bethany's silent cries break into hysteria. She has both of her hands on Laura's. Her body collapses with the next sob and her knees hit the floor. Her colorful scrubs are the only bit of life in this room. Everything else is bland, stark white, and dated.

She wouldn't like this room at all. There's nothing with any personality in it.

"Flowers. I want her to be surrounded by flowers when she wakes up." I give him the answer, but all I'm met with are sad eyes from the doctor.

"Mr. Roth," Doctor Tabor begins, pausing and breathing in deeply, but her dark brown eyes never leave mine.

I almost correct her, I almost tell her it's King, but I don't. Instead, I prepare for my rebuttal to whatever is going to come out of her mouth. The doctor is short, plain with no makeup at all, but she's determined and logical more than anything. A powerhouse in her field. Next to her is the neurologist, the one who can't look me in the eyes as the cardiologist tells me we have to prepare for the likelihood that Laura is never going to wake up.

"I understand what you said, and I know you understand what I said. I want extraordinary measures to be taken. She just needs time," I say although I lose the upper hand I have on the last line because my stern voice cracks and my eyes glaze over.

Beep, beep, beep, the steady sound of her heart beating is what keeps me going. It's steady. Her heart is a good heart. She's going to be okay now.

She finally got a good heart, so she should be able to

use it. I'll be better with this one. I won't break it. I'll make sure it never breaks if she'll just wake up.

Wake up, Babygirl, please. Wake up.

"The surgery went well," I say, giving her the words she gave me. "You said the surgery went well. All of them."

The surgeon, the one who fixed her heart, nods, and as she does, she swallows. She's frail and skinny, but something tells me it's simply the way she's built. Clasping her hands professionally in front of her buttoned-up white coat, she answers, "That's correct, the transplant went perfectly and now we monitor her to make sure her body accepts it."

"And so far?" I question.

"So far everything looks well but we need twenty-four hours to be sure.

"All of her injuries are stable and at this point we're just waiting for her to wake up, but she sustained various trauma. We lost her in surgery and she was gone for a number of minutes... and sometimes patients don't recover."

"She should have woken up by now, Mr. Roth." The neurologist speaks again, not giving me a chance to thank the other doctor who just spoke.

"She hasn't slept in days. She's just tired," I answer them and part of me really believes it. Like she's just in a deep sleep because she's exhausted from all this bullshit. God knows she needs it.

Laura's hair is pulled back with a bandage that wraps around her head. The rest of it is a messy halo on the stark white pillow. There's another bandage on her wrist that travels up to her elbow, where her arm was placed in a splint and they set the bone. But other than the bandages and the bruises, she looks like she's just sleeping. She's only resting.

"She'll wake up." My confidence forces Bethany to look at me, and I can see in her eyes that she wants to believe me but she doesn't.

No one says anything. They just stare at me.

"And what about our son?" I ask the nurse closest to me and my throat gets tight. "We will wait for her to wake up and I want to see my son."

Bethany's been quiet, her grip never loosening on Laura's hand, but her focus moves to the doctors now. She wants to know too.

"We had to intubate him as he wasn't breathing on his own. Other than that, he appears to be stable. It's a good thing that we started the steroids early, but he's still not in a good condition. The pediatrician is with him now. Statistically, every day is a better outcome, but he will be here for weeks so long as he remains stable. We have to monitor him closely and the likelihood of permanent damage is very high. His quality of life, if he does make it, is unknown at the moment."

"Can he be brought up here? So he can be with his mother?"

"Unfortunately not. Given his condition, he needs to stay where he is in the neonatal intensive care unit right now.... You should prepare yourself."

Bethany's cries are accompanied by Jase shushing her,

calmly trying to soothe her. As if words and a tender touch can heal this kind of brokenness.

"Is there anything at all I can do to help either of them?" I ask, somehow still standing on both of my feet although I know for a fact I'm shattered and everything that makes me human is on my knees, crying and begging. Yet here I stand, asking questions.

"At this point, we wait." The neurologist is the one who answers, and I hope he can feel how much I loathe him.

I hate all of them.

"You can pray, Mr. Roth." The cardiologist, a woman I didn't at all suspect to be religious, with her cold manner of speaking, offers me. She nods once, looking only at Laura before leaving us and saying one more time, "Praying is all we can do."

It's quiet for a moment, and they mumble something about leaving us alone and letting me know when I can see our son.

"Of all the ways it could happen… a fucking accident. A car crash," Bethany says and barely breathes as a suffocating sob leaves her. She buries her head in the white sheets. Her head brushes against Laura's arm and Jase is there all the while, stroking her back.

"I need to get her flowers and a different blanket," I say then clear my throat, noting how tight it is before continuing. Jase's gaze reaches mine and he doesn't have the same wounded look as all the others. "When she wakes up, I want her to smell flowers and be as comfortable as she can be."

Dropping my eyes to Laura's closed ones, I take in the bruising on her face that travels from her jaw to her neck.

When Jase makes Bethany leave, that's when I finally go to her, letting my fingers gently trail along where she's not bruised.

I kiss her head and remind myself how she hasn't been sleeping. She's only tired. That has to be it.

She's the strongest woman I know. She's only tired. There's fire in her blood and we finally have a family. "Wake up, Babygirl, we have to see our little prince. Wake up."

Beep, beep, beep.

The pediatric floor is one level below and it's silent on the walk, silent in the elevator. I pass rooms and halls, desks and plenty of other people, but all I see whenever a bed comes into view is the image of Laura, lying in that bed, her skin pale and her body motionless. The only indication that she's alive is the steady beeping of the monitors.

She can't leave me this way.

She can't do it.

She promised she wouldn't leave me. She said if it was up to her, she wouldn't. All she has to do is wake up.

It's been twelve hours and I drifted in and out for four of them. At least now I can finally see my son.

I do something I haven't done in a long damn time; I pray on the walk to pediatrics. I pray for both Laura and our son to make it. Really pray. I pray for them, and I pray for myself. If they don't live, I don't want to live either.

When we get to the glass wall with all the little carriages and babies sleeping soundly, or otherwise, I anticipate walking through those doors, but we don't.

"He's back here," a nurse tells me, her expression sympathetic. Of course my son wouldn't be in there; he's not healthy, he's not well. He isn't with the others because those babies are going to make it out of here just fine.

Tears would come easily if I wasn't so beat down already, as reality grips me. I don't stop moving, even when my throat squeezes so tight that my breath is absent. I walk steadily, listening to my footsteps and following the older woman with kind eyes and pink scrubs to the far corner of the floor, to a room without large glass panes. A room they don't want bystanders to see because it's so tragic.

There are only two other babies in this room and all of them have plastic walls covering their tiny plastic cribs. There are two with pink blankets and one with blue. So I know which one is mine.

All of them have tubes, the smallest ones imaginable. I can't stand to look at the other two children. Even when one of them moves, her little fist making a sudden motion, I see it but I can't look at her. It's crippling. They're so small and alone. It's the saddest thing there is in life.

"Here's your son," the nurse tells me, as brightly as she can although the sadness lingers there.

I take one more step forward and then another, until

my hand lays against the plastic. He's so small. So tiny I could hold him with one hand.

"Did you two have a name?"

"Not yet," I answer her and take in an unsteady breath. "We weren't expecting him so—" The words refuse to come out to finish the sentence. They stay back, choking me instead.

"If you want to sit, you can hold his hand, here." She points to a small opening in the plastic enclosure. A slot is all I have.

This is my fault. The truth is a landslide of accountability.

They're suffering for my sins and it's not fair.

None of this is fair.

He hasn't even had a full day to live. And Laura is all that is good with the world but the two of them are here in critical condition, helpless and their lives uncertain. While I get to breathe freely. Please God, don't do it to them.

It's not fair and it's all my fault.

"When we remove the tubes from his mouth, you can hold him, so long as everything is steady." I can't speak for a long time and the nurse doesn't pressure me to. Instead, I slip my pointer finger onto my son's tiny palm. And he squeezes. It's not very strong but I'll teach him. He'll get better. He'll hold on.

I have to believe that. If there's any mercy in this world…

"What is the likelihood of…" I catch myself using the word "likelihood" because that's what the doctors upstairs kept saying.

Likelihood she won't wake up.

Likelihood he won't make it past tonight.

"We're monitoring him closely and doing everything we can. If we make it through tonight, it's likely we'll be able to remove the breathing tubes. He has other issues and he won't be able to leave, but you could hold him then."

I can only nod, not trusting myself to speak.

Four days pass and it only gets harder because my confidence and hope wane. Nothing is getting better. Laura is stable but unmoving, unchanging and there's nothing we can do.

I thought, if I lay next to her, if I talked to her, if I reminded her of everything we have to look forward to, she'd wake up. If she knew her son was just downstairs, I could've sworn her eyes would open and she'd demand that I take her down there right now. And I would, God I want that more than anything.

But she doesn't respond to a damn thing. She doesn't give me any signs at all. No one knows why she doesn't wake up. *Sometimes, it just happens.* That's what they tell me and I hate them more and more with each passing day. Especially the cardiothoracic surgeon who only peers through the door. She never comes in here, but she watches and waits. I hate her the most. She was supposed to fix her, but what good is a heart if Laura can't use it?

I'm helpless with my Laura, but even more so with our baby boy.

Staring at him through the plastic box is the second-worst thing in the world.

Even yesterday, I couldn't hold him. He wasn't stable. He's a fighter, though. So is his mother but I don't know why she won't wake up.

Tonight Doctor Peters, the pediatric surgeon, said I could hold him. She said it would be good for his body to be against mine. Tummy to tummy, although really it's chest to chest. She said it's so his heart can learn to beat and I wish his mother were here. I wish Laura were here because her heart is good now, and she could do this if she were here. I know she'd love that.

"Right there is fine," she says and I take the nurse's orders of sitting down and unbuttoning my shirt. Yesterday was the first day I showered since the accident. I had to leave when the nurses all rushed in to save my son from dying and I couldn't remain. They forced me out as I screamed and demanded they save him. I had to leave the hospital for a bit; I couldn't stand to be so helpless. So I showered and packed clothes to wear. And I went back to the hospital to tell Laura she needed to wake up.

I held one of her hands in both of mine and prayed when she didn't grip my hand back. I just needed a sign, any sign. I've never cried this much. Never in my life. I've never felt this low.

The worst part is that I know this is my fault. I couldn't protect them and all I've given Laura is the consequence of my sins. I'd take it all back. All of it. I'd take it all back for them not to suffer.

What came from me praying for her to hold my hand back was a nurse three hours later telling me our son made it.

Our son.

But not Laura.

That was yesterday and today I can hold him. Doctor Peters promised me I could.

"Okay now, there are some wires here to monitor him so just be careful, all right?" She sounds more hopeful today, happy even, and I take it as a good sign as Nurse Morison sets my little prince down against me.

My hands are on him in an instant, both of them even though my fingers overlap. With the way I'm leaning back to look down at him, I'm sure he'd stay put, this tiny little baby without being held at all, but I have to hold him just to be sure he's okay.

"There we go," Nurse Morison says and quickly grabs a little blue blanket to cover him and I move one hand to hold the blanket to him, but the other is still firm against his back.

I can't move it, I can't let go, because I can feel him breathing.

From his chest to mine, I can feel his heart beating so fast. So much faster than mine.

Even when I lean down to kiss his little head, covered with a small smatter of fine dark hair, I keep my eyes on him. I can't let go and I can't look away. Today is his best day yet.

"I'll leave you be." Her voice is so quiet, I barely hear her but I hum a response and rock side to side ever so gently, watching as my little prince yawns. It's the smallest movement in the world, but it's everything.

"You've got to make it for Mommy," I whisper as I rock. How could he not make it? He's perfectly fine, this little bundle. Look at him, he's got to make it.

He's going to be okay. I know he will. He can't leave me too.

"Mommy is going to be so happy to see you when you wake up," I tell him and he wriggles against me. See, he's fine. He's healthy and fine. He's going to make it. He has to.

"I love you, little prince. When Mommy wakes up, we'll give you a name," I promise him. With my thumb stroking against the side of his little head, I tell him about Laura, about his beautiful mother and how perfect she is. I tell him how much she loves him because she can't tell him right now, but I can. "Let me tell you a story about your mother. She's a fighter like you. Even more than me, I think. She's going to be so proud of you. Probably even more proud than I am and that's… that's…" That's when I have to wipe my eyes. I don't stop rocking and I don't stop holding him though.

Not for the whole night. They let me hold him for hours and hours.

I kiss his head in between stories about Laura. And when the nurse comes back, she lets me stay, holding him to me, as she checks on him throughout the night.

The only reason I leave him at all is because sleep comes hard just before morning and they say I can't hold him if I fall asleep.

I spend the nights with Laura, holding her hand and sleeping in the small hospital bed next to her, and the days are split between our little prince and her. I tell her everything about him, from the way he makes little noises to how tight he's holding my hand now.

"He's going to make it for you, Laura, so wake up, Babygirl. Please, I love you. Wake up."

CHAPTER 18

Laura

I WOULD KNOW HER ANYWHERE FROM SEEING JUST THE back of her head, but the hoodie is what gives it away. It's bright pink but faded at her wrists, the fabric worn out so much that she poked her thumbs through the ends of her sleeves.

"Cami!" I call out to her as she's sitting on the hood of her car that she parked in the middle of the field behind the school. "You're going to get in trouble for parking out here," I yell out to her although there's a smile on my face that won't go away. It's at odds with the gloomy weather. The overcast sky threatening to rain although nothing's come down yet. I can see the storm ready to break right above us, but we're dry. So, so cold, but dry.

"Why did you park out here?" I question her like she's

lost it although she must've had a good reason to park her car in the field.

I feel light but so cold and my heart is heavy although I don't know why. Or why I'm wearing these scrubs. They're scrubs, aren't they? I do want to be a nurse one day… confusion overwhelms me, putting a deep crease on my forehead. Why the hell did I wear this to school?

"We have to get to class," I tell her, picking up my pace to get to her because I don't think she can hear me and I'm so lost right now. The tall grass tickles my legs as it slips up the loose pants. I don't remember how I got here or why we're out here. I must've hit my head hard on something. Thank God I found her.

She doesn't answer me, even when I bang my fist on the car. The metal is hard but it doesn't hurt like I expect it to. That's when I realize how quiet it is.

Is there even class? There's no one else here, no one on the roads. A shiver runs down my arms, making me cross them as I look up to Cami.

"Cami!" This time when I call her name, she looks at me, peering down from where she is on the roof of the hood of the car.

"Hey," she says, but her voice sounds so far away. There's something wrong with my hearing. There must be. I really did hit my head.

"What are you doing out here?" I question her and the wind whips away my words. I can hear each one being moved in the air, further away from Cami. I stare down the empty field, watching the overgrown grass blow as if I can see what I've just spoken hiding among the dried-out crops.

The cold slips down my spine. "We have to go inside," I tell Cami with all seriousness. There's something wrong. I can feel it. And it's far too cold to kick it out here. "Hey, let's go inside," I suggest to her again and this time my hearing is fine. It's fine. Everything is fine.

"This is where I like to stay. Sometimes Derek comes back here and if he's not here, I can still remember our first kiss right over there." She points off into the field.

"You and Derek?" I ask her, shocked and when I blink, I remember. Like a forgotten dream. "That's right!" I say and the smile grows larger on my face. "You two," I say as hope blooms but then fades and I don't know why.

I feel like I've lost days or maybe weeks. Why don't I remember?

"Come sit with me for a minute? We have some time," Cami says in an eerily calm manner but it eases something in me. I just want to talk to her, to be beside her, so I agree. Climbing on top of the car, I sit next to her but when we brush shoulders, she's so cold.

"Are you okay?"

"Oh, yeah, I'm fine, just reminiscing. It's so good to see you. You have no idea."

Something is definitely wrong. It all feels so wrong. "We should go," I warn her again. "It's going to rain and it's so cold."

"It won't rain," she tells me and smiles. Her lips are a beautiful shade of red. The color is from matching lipsticks we got together when we got our friendship rings. "I promise it won't rain."

"Hey, I got you coffee, but I think it's cold." In an instant, the surrounding environment changes to a house I don't recognize but it seems familiar. My stomach sinks and lightheadedness nearly makes me topple over. What the hell just happened? Fear chokes me and I feel sick.

We were just at the school. We were at the school.

"Cami, there's something wrong. I'm not okay." Gripping the hood of the car, I clench my teeth and try to calm the terror that rides through me. "I'm hallucinating or something."

Slowly, my eyes open and just like I thought, we're suddenly in front of a house. There's a red door. And I know I know this house. It scares me. The memories of it evade me still, but I'm terrified.

"I want to go," I say and my voice is firm this time but Cami grips my wrist with her ice-cold grasp.

The shudder that runs through me stops my heart. Or was it already stopped? I can't feel it anymore. I can't feel anything.

"I'm scared," I plead with her. I'm never scared. So little is able to scare me but I'm not okay right now, I'm not at all okay. "Something's wrong."

"I'm sorry," she says and she's quick to pull back. "I'm sorry," she repeats with less shock and more finality. "I forget sometimes."

Sitting on the edge of the car, I debate running, but my head spins and I think I'm going to be sick.

"Don't think about it right now. Don't think about that night or why you feel the way you do. Just... just talk to me please. Please. I miss you so much. Even when I see you, I miss you still."

Her light blue eyes gloss over and I get back to where I was, crawling closer to her and huddling together, my knees in my chest.

"You don't have to miss me. I'm right here," I say to comfort her even though something's wrong. I'm vigilant, looking out for whatever is coming. Something's coming, I know it.

"What's wrong?" I ask her.

"Sorry, I didn't mean to freak out. It's just that sometimes I'm so sorry."

"I don't understand." It's even colder here than it was in the field.

"Don't be scared."

"I'm terrified," I confess to her, beseeching her to get off this car and go back. Back home, back... back... I don't remember where we were.

"I don't like it here. I don't... Cami, I want to get the hell out of here," I practically yell at her but I don't mean to. "I'm just so scared."

"There's no reason to be."

"Cami, stop. This isn't funny." Trying to reason with her is... it can't be done.

"I think you should remember. Sometimes we go back to a happy place and I couldn't know what yours was. I'm so sorry."

"Remember what?" At my question, she places her hand in mine and there's warmth, the only warmth that surrounds us, but it's followed by a flood of memories.

Slowly, each one taking its time.

Bringing me back to yesterday. To the sight of my body lying in a bed.

I have to rip my hand away to hold my stomach.

"He's okay," Cami whispers. "Please," she begs me, wrapping her arm around my shoulders and I lean into her, the tears streaming down my face. "Don't leave me. It's okay. You're okay. I've just missed you so much."

Wiping my eyes haphazardly, I come to the conclusion that it's only a nightmare. Or maybe a twisted dream. I don't know what's real and what's not.

"I miss you," I manage to say, as if… if this is real, I could at least tell her that.

This is all a torturous nightmare. It has to be.

"I miss you too." She brushes her shoulder against mine again and this time it's not so cold. "At least I get to see you sometimes."

I wonder if it's her I've been seeing, the girl in the diner but as I'm thinking it, she shakes her head.

"You have to stop being so sad, you know?" Cami gives me a half smile and swings her legs down the front of the car.

"I'm not sad."

"You're a horrible liar," she tells me and I don't know why I lied to her.

"I feel so guilty," I admit. Thinking back on that day,

the day here in this house. The last time I ever saw her or it. "It was supposed to be me."

"We don't get to know fate," she tells me as if it doesn't matter. As if her dying wasn't a horrible tragedy. It was horrible and the worst thing in the world. She wasn't supposed to die. It was supposed to be me. She should have had a full life. She was sunshine in a world that desperately needs it.

I can only shake my head, everything coming back so much clearer. I want to wake up. I need to wake up from this nightmare. "I miss you so much. You'll never know how much I wish it had been me."

"You know what I was thinking all the while when I was in your house and they were hurting me?"

When she squeezes my hand, it's warm, so warm, as if she's really here with me. I hold hers with both of mine. I wish this weren't a dream. I wish this were real.

"I was hoping that you wouldn't come back home until they were gone. I'd made that decision, Laura. They thought I was you and I let them believe that. That was my choice."

It kills me to hear her say that and I search my mind for any part of me that would think she'd want that.

"It's not okay. It was supposed to be me."

"All the while I kept thinking of what excuse I would give if you walked in. How I could convince them that you were only a friend and to beg them to let me send you away. That's how I made it through it all. There were so many lies I could tell if you did come home. It was quick you know, in the scope of things."

"I'm so sorry," I whisper.

"You shouldn't be. It wasn't in your control."

Her skin looks so youthful. She hasn't aged a day, but her eyes are full of a wisdom that she didn't have before.

"Even as I was lying there dying, I prayed for you to not come home until they were really gone. Then I heard them leave and all I could think then was that I hoped Seth found me and not you or Derek. He wouldn't have let you see."

She rocks me as I hold her tight, wishing I could go back.

"You know what, though? What I'm really looking forward to?"

Wiping my eyes, I take in a shaky inhale to ask her, "What?"

"Babies and sometimes young kids can see us. Sometimes they know and I think it's because they don't know better to be scared or maybe it's because of something else I don't know. But I'm hoping he'll be able to see me."

The second she says "he," I see my son. I see a flash of him. In a little plastic box with wires attached to his chest and I gasp as I pull back from her.

I hate this nightmare. I want to wake up. Please let me wake up.

"My baby," I say and put both hands against my flat stomach and silently pray for him to kick. To tell me he's all right.

"He's all right. I've made it my mission to watch over

him." Cami smiles so bright and so wide as she adds, "He looks so much like you."

"You saw him?" I question her and a panic sets in. "I haven't held him. I need to make sure he's all right." I close my eyes tight, trying to see him again. I need to get back to him. My little prince.

"You should probably wake up; they need you."

"Come with me," I beg her and I don't know why. I know this is only a dream. One I both love and hate. One that scares me and one that I cling to. "I miss you too much."

"Hey, I'm already there. Every time you remember me, a part of me is there. It's why I like to stay in the field. Derek has the friendship ring... he knows I picked out these rings specifically because the pattern on the bands looks like the little daisy flowers on the edge of the cornfield where we first kissed, you know. It makes me laugh really. I got them for us, but anything that had to do with us always had to do with them... didn't it? It was supposed to be the four of us together forever. Did you tell him that when you gave it to him? Because he says that a lot."

"How did you know?" I question out loud how she would know that I gave the ring to Derek at the bar that night, but of course, she's only a figment of my own imagination.

She smiles knowingly and shakes her head, as if she read my mind. But of course she did.

"He started dating girls who looked nothing like me, intentionally... as if blondes aren't his type. Isn't that..."

she trails off and simply huffs then shakes her head. "He doesn't want to love again but that only makes me cry harder here. I can feel his pain." She admits that to me with tears in her eyes. "One day he'll be happy again. One day he'll love a girl and just to spite him, I hope she looks just like me," she jokes and wipes under her eyes. "He needs to love again. That's what I'm waiting for in that field. For him to tell me how he found someone. I love him too much to ever want him to be lonely. Would you tell him that? Please, tell him that."

"I'll tell him. I promise."

"I love you, babe," she whispers and then she tells me to go. I don't even get a chance to tell her I love her back before she's vanished and my world turns black.

CHAPTER 19

THERE WAS ONE RULE LAURA MADE THAT I ALWAYS followed. All the others I broke. I kept the lights on constantly, which she hated. I came home late and made too much noise. I did all sorts of shit that broke her rules.

But I never woke her up in the morning. No fucking way. I did once and I learned my lesson.

The memory makes me a huff a bit of laughter as I sit in the uncomfortable blue chair in the corner of her room. It's too small for my frame and too hard to sink into. The bags under my eyes feel heavy and exhaustion, both physical and emotional, have beat me down into a man I don't recognize.

The memory of her when she woke up before she

was ready, years ago when we were first dating, will always make me smile though. I can't help it. She's an angel, heaven sent just for me, but a demon if woken up before her alarm goes off. It's what caused her to shove me away for the first time. True bitterness from being woken up when she had twenty more minutes.

My Babygirl needed her beauty sleep. Or else she turned into a gremlin spewing curses.

So I never woke her up and if I had to, I'd sneak out of the room before she could see me. I'd never make it obvious that I was the reason she was up so I could hide from her wrath.

Another short laugh makes my shoulders shake and that warmth from the countless memories of her shuffling her bare feet while she made her way into the kitchen, desperate for coffee, mixes with profound sadness.

She looks so beautiful when I think that she's just sleeping in. She's just having a wonderful dream and she doesn't want me to wake her up.

When reality comes back though, the smile falls and there's not an ounce of warmth. It's hard to feel anything other than cold and dreadful. It kills me to see her like that. She needs to wake up. I'm dying without her.

"You have to wake up, Babygirl," I plead with her for the thousandth time. "Little prince has another surgery today." My voice tightens as I speak and I'm barely holding it together. "He did really well with the first one, you'd be proud."

They're pressuring me to give him a name. There's so

much paperwork and they said I need to do it soon, but I can't name him without her. "You have to wake up. I can't do this alone."

I sit back in the chair, wiping my eyes harshly, pretending like I'm not the shell of the man I was. "I told him you were proud and then I told him about that time you helped Derek after the surgery on his arm. You remember that?"

I keep asking her questions like one of them will do the trick. One of them will wake her up. She's going to answer one of them. She's stubborn like that. She can't let me get the last word in. That's the girl I fell in love with. She's going to answer me one of these days and I'll be so grateful for her to wake up and put me in my place.

My heel taps on the floor as I grow restless in the stiff chair. I thought the smell of flowers would do it, so I lined this room with them. Two dozen vases and then some. The windowsill is lined with them. All sorts of colorful petals from wildflowers, sunflowers, and orchids. But none of them got a reaction at all from her. I thought a kiss, a squeeze of her hand, something, anything would let her know I'm here and she should wake up.

But she only lies there, not responding to anything.

So now I talk and pretend she can hear. Sometimes I hear her answers. Maybe I'm just crazy at this point. I hope somewhere inside of her, she's listening and that she knows I keep the vases full of water and the second the flowers wilt, I get her fresh ones. I hope she can feel that I kiss her temple, then her jaw, and then her lips every morning and every night. I desperately hope she knows I'm doing the best I can with our baby boy but he's not doing so well.

He's a fighter, but he's far too young to have to fight this hard. It's not fair. It's not supposed to be this way.

"The doctors said the likelihood of survival is lower for this surgery than the first but if he makes it, then he'll have a very good shot," I say then have to pause, closing my eyes and resting my forehead in my hand, my elbow on my knee. My throat is so tight and dry. I've been through hell and still I know it's nothing compared to what he's been through. "He's a fighter like you and it was either choose not to do the surgery and say goodbye, or do the surgery and fight."

I pretend I don't hear the tears drip onto my pants and I don't feel them rolling down my overgrown stubble. "He's a fighter," I repeat, swallowing harshly and squaring my shoulders. "He's got fire in his blood like you do. You should feel the way he holds my hand." I'm here to protect her and him, because I'm supposed to be the strong one. I will be steady for them through this storm. No matter what happens in the end.

"He's going to make it," I tell her although my voice is tighter than I want. Wiping my eyes, I add, "He has you for a mom, how could he not make it through?"

My question is only answered with the click of the heater turning on. I get up to brush the back of my fingers along her cheek, making sure she's not too hot, not too cold. The salty taste on my lips is from my tears and when

I selfishly kiss her, I hope she can taste it. I hate myself for thinking it, but she never did like to make anyone upset.

I hope she knows I'm crying without her. I hope she knows I'm breaking. What good is a broken king if he doesn't have his queen? I've always been nothing without her.

"You should wake up," I whisper. "He wants to hear your voice."

"Hey." Declan's voice behind me snaps me back to reality. Brushing her hair from her face, I stand up straighter and pinch the bridge of my nose to get myself under control before turning to look at Declan. He has to know I've lost it, but he doesn't let on; he's quiet as I gather composure.

"What's going on?" I question Declan, finally turning around to see him slipping his hands into the pockets of his jeans. I should wear jeans and a black shirt like he is. They wrinkle less. Not that it would matter with the way I look. Disheveled and wrecked just the same, regardless of what clothes I wear.

"Just checking in." It's been weeks of the Cross brothers doing rotations. Jase is here a lot with Bethany and I'm grateful for it although Bethany's been breaking down more and more. It's killing her too. Three weeks is a long time for someone to not wake up from surgery. But she's going to. Our baby will make it out of surgery with flying colors and then Laura will make it out of this. I have no other choice than to believe that's the truth.

Declan stays in the doorway until I pull the chair

around the dresser and closer to the one I'm sitting in. "Have a seat," I tell him, leaning back and sucking in a steadying breath.

The constant *beep, beep, beep* never lets up as we talk.

"I found a letter in your room," Declan tells me, then reaches in his back pocket. All the while my pulse stalls and my blood turns colder, knowing he'll pull out the letter I wrote. "Care to explain it?"

He must've been snooping for something to find it. That's my first thought, but then I forget where I left it and when was the last time I even looked at it. It could have been on the fucking coffee table for all I know.

"How did you get that?" I ask as a chill lays itself across my shoulders.

"I went to your house because you need more clothes and shit."

I stare at the letter.

The deal with Marcus; the only way out. My explanation to Declan once I did what I had to do. I had to explain to make sure they understood. I knew they'd get it. They'd understand why I had to do it. They would protect her when I was gone.

I decided the day I bought the fan for little prince's room. I knew I didn't have a lot of time, so I started getting his room together. I was so sure I'd get everything done. I would have everything planned for Laura. She'd never worry again in her entire life.

"What's this about?" Declan asks.

We haven't talked business since the day of the

accident. I've been waiting for them to confront me. None of them have.

Until now.

"It's the deal I made," I confess to him, feeling a prick dance down my spine, making it harder, straighter. When his gaze meets mine, I clarify, "With Marcus."

Declan's gaze falls to the linoleum floor and I swear the heat turns off just because I said the name *Marcus.*

"He made a promise to me. He would save Laura if I killed one of the Cross brothers."

There was never a choice as to which one and Marcus knew it. Daniel, Jase and Carter have their significant others. Carter just had a baby himself. When their pictures showed, all three of them lined up, I couldn't even look at the other two. I didn't have to choose; Marcus knew because I could only look at Declan.

I tell the Cross brothers Declan is meeting at one place.

I tell Declan another.

I remember Marcus's exact words: *Pick a Cross brother to die. You do the deed.*

One of the brothers. All alone. That's the deal.

A life for a life.

"It took me a long time to find a loophole. But I did."

"And this is it?" he questions, waving the letter before tossing it down on Laura's bed. I don't like it there. Something so impure shouldn't touch her. It shouldn't be anywhere near her, so I pick it up.

"He told me to kill one of you and he'd save her. He

promised he'd save her first, so… so as far as the deal goes, it's nonexistent. None of it matters anymore."

"But this letter?" Declan questions.

"As far as I could tell, the only reason he'd have me do it, was so that the remaining brothers would kill me. I'm sure it was a test in one way or another. I couldn't see clearly; all I could think about was Laura." Just saying her name makes me close my eyes and grip the armrests. I would do anything for her. "I could have told you but then he said he would stop the motions that had started that would save Laura. I couldn't tell anyone. I was trapped. So I agreed."

"But this letter?" he repeats, more anger and impatience showing.

"I could never kill you. I could kill myself, but then he'd go after Laura. He said he'd be there to make sure it was me so it had to take place. I lied to him and said I'd do it." My gaze shifts from Laura to Declan as I confide in him. "But I wanted you to kill me instead."

"So… once Laura was well and Marcus had done his part, I planned to give you the address like he told me to. I'd go, I'd lift my gun and when I fired the blanks, you'd kill me. I would honor my deal with Marcus and by that point, Laura would be safe and healthy. And I wrote the letter with the intent of sending it the day of the meet. That way you'd all know the truth, so you'd protect Laura in case Marcus didn't feel that I held up my end as best as I could. You couldn't know. If you knew, he'd know. I didn't see another way."

"You thought I'd kill you?" he asks me with a dull tone, not even looking at me.

"If I raised a gun to you? If I fired?" I pause, feeling all the agony of my decision again. "I knew you would. I had to leave you the letter so you knew it was only to save Laura. She had a life here before I came back into it. She was happy. She loved it. She would find that again. I didn't want you to carry the weight that you'd shot me. It was my decision and I needed you all to still love her. To still protect her—"

"You were ready to die."

"To protect her? To end all of the bad shit in her life that follows her because of me?" As I speak, my voice raises and I hate myself even more. Whenever we're together, bad shit rains down on her. It was the only choice. She was happy once without me; she'd be happy again. One day. And I would have everything prepared for her. All the money I've made, plus the house would be set up for her and our little boy. The Cross brothers would protect her because they'd owe me. She would be safe forever. It would have been worth it.

"All of this is because of me. I'd leave her the money and everything she'd ever need. You'd protect her. There are more of you than there are of me and I've already failed her so many times. She would finally be safe." Maybe he doesn't understand because he doesn't love someone like I love her.

"If I'm not there… it was the solution to everything. And then this happened."

"You could have just killed me," he offers, looking dejected as he stares at Laura's motionless body hidden under the chenille throw from the living room.

"I could never kill you." My throat's tight just thinking about that. "You and Jase … you're family… you guys are the only friends I have. The only semblance of a family I've known for years."

I try to lighten it up and my next comment gets a huff of a laugh from Declan. "Besides, if I did that, your brothers would kill me…" The half-smile on my face that matches his falters when I add, "And then she wouldn't be protected. There are more of you than there are of me. And a family. A real family." The last part hurts the most. She deserves that. She's never had one, not since her grandmother died, but she has one now. I couldn't take that away from her. "Our son deserves that too."

"You're talking like you aren't a part of our family. Like you're not one of us. When did that change? When did you decide to leave?"

"When the idea of killing you was something I actually considered." Looking him in the eyes, it's hard to admit it. "It was only a moment, but I considered it. I don't deserve to be your family and—"

"Bullshit." He's quick to cut me off with a venom I don't anticipate. "You don't get to just leave. You're still like a brother to me."

"I'm sorry," is all I can say, truly feeling like less of a man.

"So, that? That's what you were going to do?" he asks

me in a tone that makes me sick as he points to the folded letter.

"A life for a life. That was the deal. Mine for hers is what I decided." I lean closer to him, making sure he looks me in the eye as I add, "I'd make that deal any day."

He shakes his head, staring at me like he doesn't even know me. "And here I thought you were coming to terms with killing me," he says as his expression changes to one of sympathy and sorrow, "not that you were coming to terms with your own death."

Beep, beep, beep.

The monitor is steady as I process what he's saying.

"We wired the warehouse before you went in. We couldn't let you go alone, and we had arranged for backup. We were ready to protect you if anything happened."

"You knew?" Disbelief shows in my tone. Betrayal creeps in.

"Yes, of course we did. And Marcus knows we wired it because once you left, he told Walsh he had to stop the eavesdroppers and everything went out."

"You knew this whole time." I can't fucking believe it. My hand scrubs down my face. "You fucking knew?" I snap at him, hating them for putting me through this shit when I was already suffering. I fucking died more and more every day keeping it all to myself.

"Carter wanted to know what you'd do. I told him you wouldn't go through with it." His tone holds condolences. "I knew you wouldn't."

"I can't breathe."

"Did you think we didn't know?"

"How would I ever think you'd know?" I practically sneer, betrayal but also relief running through me.

"He played you."

"And he didn't save her." The words are torn from me. "That was all that mattered. And he didn't save her." My anger doesn't mean shit. The reality is that it didn't happen. In another life, in an alternate story, I died to save her. But this is what's real. I'm alive and she's… *Please, Babygirl, wake up.*

"I'm sorry." Declan's words are the sincerest he's been since he stepped into the room. His hand lands on my shoulder. "She's going to make it."

It's quiet for a moment and I take the time to lean forward and hold her hand. As my thumb brushes against her knuckles, I keep praying she'll squeeze my hand.

Any sign. I just need any sign.

"I came here to tell you I got a note from Marcus."

Hate mixes with absolute contempt in my blood. I let her hand go, unwilling to hold her while I feel like this. He was supposed to make her better. Instead, now she's here. I would have given him more for him to do it faster. Why didn't he help her? He said he could help her.

"He wants to meet with me. Doesn't say why. Just lists an address and a time."

"I guess this is his backup plan," I snidely comment.

On the edge of my vision, Declan shrugs. "If he wanted me dead, he could easily do it."

My gaze doesn't move from Laura's lips, down to the curve of her neck.

"I never should have made a deal with him." I finally look at Declan. "I never should have said I'd help him with shit."

"You did what you had to do."

"Hey." The sound of Jase's voice comes in along with a knock.

"You're supposed to knock first," Declan reprimands him although it lacks strength.

Jase glances at Laura but not for long. He never looks at her for long. I know what he's thinking: She's already gone.

Pulling up the final chair in the room, he drags it over to where we are and sits with us.

But first he puts a vase on the windowsill. A single rose in a simple vase. I take that time to calm down as best I can.

I watch him and I know he can see the question in my eyes. "She didn't have any red roses in here. I thought a red rose… you should get her roses."

He clears his throat as he sits down.

"You talk to him?" he asks Declan and he nods in response.

"Good," is all Jase gives him in response.

Looking past Declan I question him, "You aren't going to ask him what I said? What I was going to do?"

He shakes his head and says, "I don't need to. I know you'd never do it."

Struggling to feel deserving of his trust, I press my back to the chair and sit there, my elbows on my knees, my hands clasped in front of me.

"You might think we don't know you, Seth King. But we know you. All of us do. And you'd never betray us."

"I feel like I betrayed her." I can't help but give the statement just under my breath. She was supposed to be safe with me, and I couldn't protect her.

"Bethany's with little prince," Jase comments, thankfully changing the conversation. "Did you think of a name for him?"

Emotions make my answer tight as I say, "I'm waiting for her to wake up."

I can't look at them when I say that, because then they'd see the doubt that breaks my chest in half as I look at her.

"Don't get mad."

I lift my gaze to Declan's, ready to tell him if he feels the need to lead with that, then he knows I'm going to be pissed.

"I just want to make sure we're on the same page," he emphasizes, his hands in the air in a defensive gesture.

"If… if Laura doesn't wake up and little man downstairs is released… He's with us, right? He's not going anywhere even if… Laura…." He has the decency not to finish.

"He's my son," I answer him adamantly with an edge of a threat.

"Of course." Jase is quick to agree with me and Declan follows suit.

"I know, I know. I was just making sure we're on the same page is all. Same plan. We stick to the same plan as before."

"Regardless of what happens, I'll take care of him. I'll be the father Laura would have wanted me to be."

I don't like talking about her like she's not here anymore, when she's right in front of us.

I have to cover my face with my right hand to keep from fucking crying. It's all I can do to hold myself together.

"Hey." Jase keeps talking, like I'm not entirely breaking down. "You know adopted kids, they say they look like their adopted parents. It's because of the facial expressions. When you're around someone so much, you start to mimic the way they say things, do things, it's what makes a person a person. So even though… biologically speaking, he's… you know. He could still look like you and no one would ever know."

It takes a long time for me to even breathe, let alone think about what Jase just told me. I know his intent was to make me feel better or distract me, but all I can think of is that in that picture, Laura's not there.

After a long moment, I tell them, but I plead with Laura, holding her hand in both of mine. "He can't be left with just me."

CHAPTER 20

Laura

I'M IN AND OUT. IT'S THE FIRST TIME I'M AWARE OF IT. Aware of the fact that I'm in a hospital bed. Although it smells like I'm in a field of wildflowers. It's wonderful, but I want to see Seth; I want to hold my son. I keep hearing bits of his voice in the distance and they're talking about little prince. I just want to open my eyes so badly.

Trying to wake up has never been so difficult.

I struggle to listen and sometimes it's easy, sometimes it's all black. I'm not falling though, not anymore. There's no dip in my stomach, no wind rushing around me. I'm simply still. Motionless. Waiting and unable to do anything but struggle to listen.

Sometimes it's Bethany's voice, sometimes it's Seth. Sometimes it's the nurses like it is today.

What are they saying? I swear my eyebrows pinch; I can feel it happening. *Just wake up!* Frustration is overwhelming until I hear their conversation.

"I'm telling you." A hissed voice is hushed as she speaks. "It's the sweets."

My fingers move, I know they do. It's only a centimeter at most. But they moved. *Wait, what did they say?*

"For the love of God, it was just a vial in her pocket, there was none of it in her system."

Are they talking about me? I didn't have a vial in my pocket.

"That was a good heart," the second voice says. I got a heart. I have a heart. A wave of warmth flows through me from head to toe. Disbelief and elation swarm through me. The steady beeping corresponds to the pounding in my chest. I wish I could feel true relief, but I'm so scared that I can't move, and I can't speak. I'm terrified every time this happens… unless Seth is here. *Where's Seth?*

"She killed herself on the table." The comment is made harshly. All I can do is try to move my fingers again. *Please, move, some part of me move.*

"I still can't believe she did that. I can't believe that poor woman killed herself."

What? No I didn't. I try to swallow so I can scream at the woman making accusations that aren't true but it's so dry it hurts. Fuck, it all hurts. Writhing is futile, there's no escape from my still state.

"She tried to kill herself before even being on that table…"

"I don't understand why. I liked her. She was so sweet, always bringing in the hats for the babies and the random flowers."

I stop trying to do anything but listen to them.

"I was shocked too but then I got to thinking, why was she always here? For months that blonde was hanging out on the benches at the park constantly. She'd be in the lobby all the time…" The one nurse's voice trails off.

"You know she was troubled and she was mourning." The second nurse's tone is riddled with remorse.

The first female voice, the skeptic who first brought up the sweets, says, "I think she'd decided she was going to kill herself here and she was just waiting for the guts to do it."

"Then why do it at a hospital where we could save her if she really meant it? It doesn't make sense."

"I'd like to believe she didn't want to die, but when she did it on the table…."

"Well either way, it's a bloody miracle she did it when she did."

"And how she did it… if she had bled out, that heart wouldn't have been any good."

"I don't want to talk about this. It's too much."

"That's too much? Of everything you've seen."

"Just stop… what's her pulse?"

"It's high."

"Give her more meds."

"You know they say she's one of them."

"What?"

"The blonde girl… the one whose heart this one got.

The one with the sweets in her pocket. Maybe God didn't want anyone else to have that heart. And that's why she's not waking up."

"One of them? Like one of… Marcus's?" I barely hear her when she whispers, but still the goosebumps run down my arms. Do they see it? Can they tell that I can hear them? *I can hear you!*

"Yes. You know she is. One of the troubled ones."

"No, we don't know that. As far as I know, that man, Marcus, doesn't even exist. She was a sad woman who lived a horrible life and went through hell. She didn't want to go through it anymore. That's all. And luckily, she happened to end her life the moment that this woman needed her heart. Like I said, it's a bloody miracle."

"What the hell are you two doing?" A third voice interrupts the morbid conversation.

A woman killed herself… she killed herself and I got her heart as a result? If I was capable, I'd be sick. I'd be physically sick. Everything processes slowly. A blonde who hung out. A blonde who was waiting to kill herself.

As it stands, I'm merely lightheaded and feeling the edge of my world turn cold and dark.

Their conversation is barely audible and only pieces are heard.

The blonde girl.

The sweets.

Why isn't she waking up?

I hear them, but I can't answer. I can't question them. A blonde girl. For the longest time, all I can see, all I can think about is Cami. But when sleep pulls me under, I remember the girl in the coffee shop. The girl who looked so much like her. The girl who gave me chills.

I hope I remember when I wake up. But the conversations blur and the next time I'm in and out, I don't remember anything, but I can move my fingers that much more.

Beep, beep. My head hurts. My body's stiff.

When I open my eyes, all I want to do is rub the tired ache from them but I can barely move my arm. It feels as if I've run a marathon and I can't even stand power walking. Everything is so damn sore.

Rolling my head to the side, I feel the groan before I hear it leave me.

Fuck, it all hurts.

"Miss Roth, Miss Roth," I hear someone say. The voice is peppy and comes from my right. "I'm Nurse Hale."

My blurry vision comes into focus to show me a young brunette woman, her hair pulled back in a simple ponytail. Her blue scrubs are loose on her. She's a tiny little thing and her feminine tone matches her aesthetic.

"Water." Before the word is even fully out of my mouth, I hear her pour a cup of it but then she's frantic, looking for a straw.

"A straw, a straw… she's up! Page neurology." I don't know who she tells the last part to, but she's in my face with a plastic straw and I greedily suck it down.

It smells like flowers. Like heaven. As I pull my knees up, stretching my aching muscles, I feel my chenille throw, my favorite throw from the sofa and I pull it close to me, smelling it. It usually smells like Seth. Like his cologne or his body wash. Right now it doesn't and my chest feels hollow.

"Seth," I say, whispering his name, feeling the loss and suddenly very scared to be in a hospital.

"He's here, he's just waiting downstairs. Let me get him for you," she says and the nurse rushes her words out, obviously excited but I reach up, gripping her arm.

"Wait," I say and my heart races, but it's different. It's a steady gallop. "What happened?"

The smile slips from the nurse's pretty face.

"Do you know who you are?" she asks me.

"Laura Roth." She nods at my answer, holding my hand and taking a seat on the edge of my bed.

"And do you know where you are?"

"Hospital. I know... I know I was waiting on a transplant... I..." The memories come back slowly. Delilah... the accident. "I was hit by a car."

"Yes, and you suffered a number of injuries, most of them minor and healed now. In the process you also got a heart transplant."

"And my baby?" I ask and my voice is strained. My hands pressed to my stomach that's obviously flat. My eyes are watery.

"He's downstairs, survived the delivery, had an immediate surgery and then two more. He's a trooper and a sweet, happy, healthy baby boy."

"He's healthy?" Overwhelming emotions force me to cover my mouth. As she nods, all I can think is that we made it. We're okay. We're all okay.

"It was a rough road, a bit touch and go for him at first, but he's much better now." She continues, "Your… significant other, Seth, is downstairs with him in pediatrics as we speak. I'll go tell them you're awake."

Before she can stand, I tell her to wait. "I just… I need a minute."

"I understand. You've been in here for quite some time. It's been almost a month."

A month. That knowledge is crushing. I've been in here for a month? My hands shake and I cover my face again, lifting my legs up and holding my knees to my chest.

"The doctors will be in shortly to make sure everything's all right."

I can only nod, my forehead resting against the blanket. The sweet nurse rubs my back the entire time.

"The important thing is that you got a new heart, the surgery went well, and now you're all right. We were worried you weren't going to wake up."

As I sit there, gathering my composure and swallowing down the fact that a month of my life is gone, my baby boy is here, and I have a steady heartbeat, little memories start to come back. Overheard conversations.

"You were very lucky that a heart happened to become available when you were brought in. If someone had planned it, it couldn't have been more perfect timing."

A distant memory comes back. A conversation.

"From the blonde who killed herself."

"What?" The shock in her voice makes me raise my gaze to the wide-eyed woman.

"I heard you talking. Or your friend. I don't remember." My head hurts and I need more water. She holds it for me, apologizing profusely for her lack of professionalism.

"You couldn't have known that I could hear."

"I'm so sorry, Miss Roth." She looks mortified.

"I won't tell anyone," I offer her with a smile and then take another large gulp. "Who is she? The woman?"

"I didn't know her personally."

"But you knew of her? A few of you did."

"She was a troubled woman, about your age. She'd been in before for overdose; it was an attempted suicide. And then she hung around outside and donated baby blankets she'd crocheted. She was here a lot... and then when you came in, it wasn't even ten minutes later that she arrived and tried to cut herself out front. We brought her in and before we could do anything..."

She doesn't finish, but I remember what the one nurse said. "She cut her throat open."

"Yes. There was no way to save her. It wasn't a cry for help." Her somber voice drops even lower. "She was just ready to go. And she happened to be a match for you, so..."

"I'm freezing," I comment to change the subject and pull the throw around my shoulders. I feel awful for the poor girl. Benefiting from her sadness feels so wrong.

"Hey... she may have died, but she was able to save you. And that's a beautiful silver lining if ever there was one."

All I can do is force a tight smile. "I am happy to be alive."

"You're not the only one... do you want to see your baby?"

CHAPTER 21

Seth

"**O**NE TIME, WE'D ONLY BEEN DATING FOR…" I rack my memory, trying to place the moment as I rock in the chair. Our little boy likes to hear stories about us. In the last few weeks I've learned the more I talk to him, the longer he sleeps. So I tell him stories and our little prince naps in between bottles. Three more days of him doing this well, and we'll be able to leave. It's both the best news and the worst, because Laura still hasn't woken up.

I only tell him the good parts to make sure he has the sweetest dreams and it helps me too, to remember all the moments in my life with Laura. They are the best memories I have.

I let my nose fall to his little head, where his soft baby

hair tickles my nose as I kiss his noggin. Turning my cheek to his head so my breath doesn't disturb him, I tell him, "We'd been dating for a few months. Back then, your mommy didn't want to believe I loved her. And I know I didn't love her as much as I do now, but I swear I did. She was strong and beautiful and even though I knew I wasn't good enough for her, I still wanted to kiss her because I thought it would make her happy and I wanted so badly to make her happy."

My voice breaks for a moment and I close my eyes, rocking him. It happens sometimes, when the reality creeps in and the overwhelming sadness keeps me from being able to tell him the good parts.

"She loved me though. I could feel it. There's this little piece inside of you," I whisper as I rock him in the nursery. It's only the two of us in this room. "There's something inside of you and it tells you where to go. It always led me to your mommy, little prince. And I could feel it, I could see it in your mother's eyes. She felt it too. So I knew if I waited long enough, she'd always come back to me."

I open my eyes so they stay dry. They're sore and bloodshot from not being able to sleep. How can I? When any moment she's going to wake up for us. I know she will. She has to.

Swallowing thickly, I get back to my story, to the good part that our son needs to hear.

"This one time, she nearly said it. She almost said 'I love you' even though she wouldn't even call me her boyfriend. Your mother... she's a stubborn girl with a wild spirit but she's so good to the ones she loves. She's the best of any person I ever met and she loves so hard. She loves you. If she could tell you that now she would. She's the kind of person who says it every day even when she's angry. Even when she doesn't know if it'll last or if she'll hear it back.

"She said it first and she told me all the time but I never said it back to her. I waited too long. Little prince, when you fall in love, you should tell the girl. Even if you don't know if she'll say it back. Or else you'll end up like me, remembering all the times she said it and that moment she almost did where I wish I had said it instead of just kissing her."

I almost ask him to promise me, but then I realize how ridiculous I am. This little life can't promise me anything; I'm the one who should be making every promise to him.

"I'll tell you every night just like she would have… like she will, I mean." My throat gets tight and I take a moment to calm myself before promising him, "You'll get all the good I have, little man. I'll give you everything in the world and I'll tell you every night too. I love you. Your mom loves you. And there's so much love there from her, it'll protect you always. We'll make it, you and me, because she loves us so much we don't have a choice but to do otherwise. That's what love does. That how strong it is. So when you feel it, say it, let them know. Something as strong as that shouldn't be kept secret. I promise you I'll show you that. I'll prove it to you."

I'm too busy talking to my son to see Nurse Morison in the doorway. But the moment I see her, I know something's changed. My heart doesn't beat until I grasp it fully.

"Mr. King, she's awake."

CHAPTER 22

Laura

I'LL NEVER FORGET THE LOOK ON SETH'S FACE. EVEN as I'm torn between the two, my small little prince wrapped up tight in a blue and white blanket, and the man I've loved my whole life.

I'll never forget the relief and gratitude in his piercing blue eyes or the way his throat tightened and his strong jaw trembled just slightly as he whispered my name.

"Seth." I wanted to say his name with strength but the single syllable is lost in a sob. My hands tremble as I reach up to him, the moment he closes the distance in only seconds.

His collared shirt, normally ironed and smooth, is a rumpled mess. The top buttons are undone, revealing his skin underneath. His pants look like he's slept in them.

The sight of him like this, a complete mess, my Prince Charming who's been through hell and back, somehow living to tell the tale… that's the sight before me. My hero. Forever my hero even in a life where the villains go unseen and there is no happily ever after in sight.

The gasp that comes from me is unexpected, but so is the sight of my baby boy's face. His eyes are closed but he yawns and it's the sweetest thing I've ever seen in my life.

Seth is gentle, ever so gentle when he lays my baby boy in my arms. My body rocks, my eyes close but only for a moment, only so much so that I can feel the overwhelming reprieve and devotion that envelops me. I have never felt like this. Safe and at peace. Seth's stubble brushes my jaw when he kisses my cheek. It's rough and comes with a wave of warm air that smells like him. That masculine smell that waits for me in the early morning on his pillow. The scent that comes with memories and sentiments of affection. It's either that smell or the tender touch of his lips on my skin that brings mine to his in a heated embrace.

His lips mold to mine, brushing against them and then deepening. I can barely breathe; I can barely do anything but try to convince myself that this is real.

I get to live. I get to have the love of my life. And we get to keep our child.

The small sound of our baby boy interrupts the kiss and I hold my son closer to me. He's so tiny, engulfed in the blanket and nestled against my chest. His little hands gripping the cloth between the two of us so tight. All I want in this world is to protect him, to make sure he lives the most blessed of lives. I will do everything I can so that he doesn't live like we did. His life will be so much more than a series of tragic mistakes and running from the past.

"He looks like you." That's the first thing Seth says to me. With a broad smile on his face as his head falls in the crook of my neck and his hand slips around my waist. I hold on to our son and he holds on to me. Leaning my head against his, his hot tears leave a wet trail in the crook of my neck.

"We'll give you two a minute," Nurse Hale offers us, polite and only speaking loud enough to be heard as the two of us lose ourselves in the moment.

We made it out alive. All of us. It's a miracle and I'll never take a second for granted. I'll never run again because this is all I want. Seth King and our little prince.

"We're okay?" I question Seth the moment the door to the hospital room shuts. Brushing the tear from under my eye and glancing down at our baby and then back to me, Seth nods, his expression adamant for the first time since he walked in here. "We're better than okay," he answers me, never breaking our gaze.

My inhale is shaky at best, not knowing how it's possible, but grateful that I got my happily ever after.

"I love you," I say, getting out the words just before Seth takes my head in his hands, giving me a searing kiss and then resting his forehead against mine.

"I love you too," he whispers and kisses the tip of my nose.

He wipes under his own glossy eyes, staring at our baby boy while he reaches behind him to drag a chair closer to the hospital bed.

"When can we leave?" A gruff laugh leaves him at my question. "I just want to go home with you and him."

"Well, we should probably name our son first," he says as his large hand takes my free one and then with his other hand, he strokes the side of our baby's face.

My son's closed eyes scrunch, as if he doesn't want to wake up and my baby wriggles in my arms.

"He's so much bigger now," Seth says with reverence and the admission tightens a vise around my heart. I remember what the nurse said. A month. I missed the first month of my son's life.

"Is he…?" I trail off as my bottom lip wobbles ever so slightly.

Seth's answer is everything that I need. "He's perfect."

He never stops stroking the side of our baby's head as I gently rock him, not wanting to disturb him.

"He had to have a few surgeries and he was a champ through all of them." As Seth talks, my inhales come in shaky and it takes everything not to cry even harder. I could drown in the sadness of what we've been through, or I can rock my perfect baby to sleep while the man I love tells me he loves me too.

I choose the latter.

"He loves to hear stories and I swear he knows your

name," Seth says and I look into his blue eyes, shining with devotion as he looks at the sweet bundle in my arms. I never stop rocking as he tells me our little man stops crying when Seth says, "Laura." He pauses, like he's waiting for the rest and Seth swears if he tells him some mushy story from when we first got together, he stops crying. He wants to hear the good stuff, that's what Seth says.

Most importantly, he says so many times how much he loves us, the three of us.

I love us too. I love all of us and although it hurts how we got here; I'm so grateful that we did get here. This is all I ever wanted. To love and be loved and share that love with our little prince.

"Can we name him Cameron?" I ask Seth. Judging by the way he peers at me, with long-ago memories in his eyes, I think he knows why. "I just feel like…" My throat's tight and I want to cry just thinking about Cami.

I don't remember much, barely anything at all really. A month went by and all I did was sleep. There's some part of me though that feels like she was holding my hand. Like I wouldn't have gotten through any of this without her. Maybe I just miss her that much. Maybe there's more to it, I don't know. "I just want to remember her always and honor her in a way… is that… I don't know. It's—"

"I love it," Seth says, cutting me off, kissing my cheek and preventing me from crying even more. "Yes. Yes, let's name him Cameron."

CHAPTER 23

Seth

"Y OU'RE GROWING SO FAST," I SAY AND MY words are lost since they're whispered to a sleeping baby boy. Even though he's dreaming, he holds my thumb with all his might. His wrists are chubby, his cheeks full. He's gaining weight and the pediatrician is happy with his progress.

We're in the clear. It took three more days after Laura's release, but we're finally able to breathe now that we're in the clear.

I never knew how much relief those words would bring me, doctors telling us we can all go home. Bring *us*.

"I love it when he holds my fingers like that." Laura's comment is gentle and comes from the open door to the nursery.

In only her silk robe that clings to her curves, she tempts me like she never has. Seeing her with our baby boy, little Cameron, makes me ache for her.

I'm already hard by the time her eyes move from Cameron to my gaze. She must know because even with only the faint light from the hallway behind her, I can see her blush rise up from her cheeks to her temple.

"You're impossible," she huffs humorlessly, wrapping her arms around her front. Her bare feet pad on the floor as she comes to me, although I know it's only to scoop up Cameron into her arms.

We have another week before sex is an option. I am counting down every fucking hour.

She teases me even more, taking Cameron from me, but settling down into my lap. With my arms wrapped around her, I keep her close to me, smelling her fragrant hair as I sigh easily.

I never knew how badly I wanted this. Her with me and a child too. A family.

It's more important than anything else, which is why I'm continuing to lay low, only running the bar for the Cross brothers... indefinitely. I don't ever want Laura or our son mixed up in anything else. So I took a step back and everyone was on board with that.

"I want a million more," I comment and with my admission, our little prince stirs in Laura's arms.

She only laughs, soft and easy. Her shoulders shake against my chest with it and then she rocks Cameron. I expect her to joke about another being too much or that

I'm just ridiculous. She doesn't though. "I do too," she whispers.

"Could you not sleep?" I ask her.

"I got six hours straight," she answers with a smile and then looks deep into my eyes, still rocking our baby as she adds, "I dreamed I was missing you two."

A soft hum leaves me, vibrating down my chest and she snuggles in closer to me.

As much as I love this, as much as I want to live in this moment forever, I know what day it is.

The reminder makes me hold Laura closer to me. I kiss her temple, her hair tickling my nose when I do, trying not to think about what's going on outside these walls.

I want to stay here forever with her. In love with her and loved by her.

Declan told me it was all right. He said the note told him he had to go alone and there was nothing I could do. Still, I want to know what happens. I need to know this shit with Marcus is over. Forever.

I got my happily ever after, but I don't know at what cost.

"You all right?" Laura's question brings me back to this moment and it's then that I realize my heart is racing with fear for Declan.

"Fine," I lie to her and kiss the tip of her nose. She shouldn't worry, not when I don't know what to tell her.

"I love you, Laura," I tell her rather than confess my fear. "I would do anything for you."

She has no idea how much I mean it. I'd sacrifice everything for her.

"I know," she answers with a soft smile on her lips as Cameron coos in her arms. "I love you too."

"You need to sleep," I comment, noting how our little prince is falling asleep in her arms. "Let him sleep and you get into bed."

"I'm not tired," she protests and I'd smack her ass if it wasn't firmly in my lap right now.

"You will be when I'm done with you," I whisper at the shell of her ear. Her eyes close and her breath hitches.

"But we can't—"

"I know what we can and can't do," I say, cutting her off. "I'm far too aware."

As quiet as can be, she sets our son down in his crib, giving him one last look before peering back at me. She catches me standing up and her gaze goes straight to my cock. I'm so fucking hard for her. I take my time closing the distance, watching that rosy color in her cheeks grow.

Cupping her cheek in my hand, I press my lips to hers and then give her one last warning. "Get your ass on that bed, Babygirl."

I don't have to swat her ass, because she immediately turns around, making her way to our bedroom. I do anyway though, a slap that makes her gasp that sweet sound. The smile's wide on her beautiful face and there's a happiness and a lightness in her step that I haven't seen in so long.

She's mine forever like this. And I'll make damn sure it stays that way.

Marcus

He came alone like I knew he would.

The youngest of the Cross brothers has always been the most trusting. He doesn't remember the events of his past like the others do. He didn't have to go through it like they did. That's the only explanation I have for his trust in me.

He shouldn't trust me. No one should. Just like I don't trust a damn one of them.

Seth didn't trust me either, but he sure as hell was willing to make a deal.

He may think I didn't follow up on our arrangement, oh, but I did.

Little Audrey, with her long blonde hair, would have killed herself so many times before. She begged for death and her tragic story pleaded for me to let her let go in the years I've known her. In an effort to convince her otherwise, an effort for her to see the greater good, I told her she couldn't do it, unless her death became someone else's miracle.

It worked for a while… until she happened upon Laura. She found a picture online of two girls. One that looked like her and the other was Laura Roth.

She was too wise for her age. Finding Laura and knowing she could save her was the way out she'd been hunting for years. *She said it was a sign.*

It certainly gave me leverage, but if I could have saved Audrey, I would have. I tried. Some souls are just too far gone.

Audrey's death, her suicide, hurt me more than anyone would ever know, even if she did save a life.

Seth got what I promised him and it killed me to allow it, to tell Audrey the moment I knew about the accident. But I won't hold him to our deal. It wasn't for him anyway. It was a test of his dear friend.

Declan steps closer to a stone carved with his own last name on it. His brother's first. The dried leaves beneath his feet crack and crumble.

Declan came to me for this. He came months ago wanting something I didn't know if he deserved… So I tested him.

No man would allow the woman he loves to die. Seth could never say no. He would have done anything for her. I allowed Declan to know. I let them plant the wires, I let them listen in as I offered the deal.

He knew his best friend was made an offer he couldn't resist. Declan knew Seth had to kill him in order to save the woman he loved.

After seeing what happened…

Declan deserves what he asked for and I'll give it to him.

I do have regrets, for the pain it put Seth through, but that's on Declan. Not on me. All of these men, they want, want, want, but I have never gotten what I wanted. Not until now.

Snow gathers in the sky, making it a cloudy gray to blanket the darkening evening. The chill is biting and it reminds me of the night everything changed for me.

The night I met her.

A stream of light descends between us and it casts his shadow long against the stone and grass that litter the graveyard. More importantly, the light gleams from the metal in his hand.

I'm certain his gun is loaded. Maybe he has less trust than I thought he did.

No matter. If he thought I'd let it end like this, he thought wrong.

"Declan." I call out his name before he can leave. His back is to me, his shoulders tight and tense. So at odds compared to my easy posture.

He doesn't turn around, which only brings the corners of my lips up into a smirk.

"I have one last deal to offer." One more. Because I have to. "I know something you don't. Something you really, desperately want to know."

"What is it?"

"Turn around, Declan."

"Are you going to kill me?"

"No," I answer him and a nervousness rolls up my spine, coupled with a sickness in my stomach. It's been so long since someone's learned who I am.

It's a risk, but one I have to take. I need to for her.

She begged me for this.

Declan's slow to turn and face me. The recognition lights in his eyes, his expression turning from stone to one of confusion and then quickly, betrayal.

I give him a moment and he speaks a single word. "You?"

Marcus's story is up next.

For an extended epilogue of Laura and Seth's story, sign up for my newsletter. Spoiler alert, she got a baby shower, even if it was a little late. xoxo

ABOUT THE AUTHOR

Thank you so much for reading my romances. I'm just a stay at home mom and avid reader turned author and I couldn't be happier.

I hope you love my books as much as I do!

More by Willow Winters
www.willowwinterswrites.com/books